A heartwarming story of forgiveness and redemption! There were moments that I laughed out loud, and moments that I was brought to tears. A wonderful story, and a great reminder of God's love and the work He is doing in our lives.

— STEPHANIE M. ~ AMAZON CUSTOMER

This is such a heartwarming romance. I enjoyed it from beginning to end, and I'm looking forward to more from this author!

— M. H. ~ AMAZON CUSTOMER

A Summer in Shady Springs is a sweet story of redemption and romance. It was hard to put down! Right now, when the world seems so dark and sad, this is a perfect read to remember the all-important hope we have in Christ (and the fun and joy of being young and in love, too!).

— KRISTEN B. ~ AMAZON CUSTOMER

A Summer in Shady Springs

Shady Springs Book One

Sarah Anne Crouch

Scrivenings
PRESS
Quench your thirst for story.
www.ScriveningsPress.com

Published by Scrivenings Press LLC
15 Lucky Lane
Morrilton, Arkansas 72110
https://ScriveningsPress.com

Printed in the United States of America

Paperback ISBN 978-1-64917-444-4

eBook ISBN 978-1-64917-445-1

Second Edition. This book was previously published in 2021 by Anaiah Press. The publishing rights were transferred to Scrivenings Press LLC in 2024.

Cover design by Linda Fulkerson—www.bookmarketinggraphics.com

For my mom, without whom this book
would not exist. You are my hero.
Thank you for believing in me.
I love you big!

*M*adeleine pursed her lips in thought. I really don't want to do this. She rose from the table to refresh her coffee and

reflected over the email she'd just received.

Congratulations on your finished painting for the hospital! Your mom sent lots of pictures, and I think it's absolutely beautiful!

I know you are very busy and important nowadays, but I was hoping you might still have time for your favorite Aunt Clara.

Our church is wanting to put a mural outside of our new children's wing, and I immediately thought of you. I showed some of your pieces to the elders, and they agreed your style is exactly what we want.

We wouldn't be able to pay much, but I can throw in free room and board! Please let me know as soon as you decide. And even if you say no, I still want you to visit your poor old aunt very soon.

Aunt Clara might have tired to disguise her motives, but a job for the church was simply too convenient. Returning to that town, working for those people, might be more than Madeleine could handle.

She settled down to type a refusal, but the longer she sat, the harder it was to come up with a decent excuse. She was finished with her latest project and didn't have anything terribly pressing to work on—nothing that paid, at least, except a part-time job waiting tables at a BBQ restaurant in downtown Kansas City. And money was important. Ever since Madeleine had moved back in with her mother after college, she'd been actively saving for a down payment on her own place, but the starving artist stereotype wasn't too far from Madeleine's reality. She should jump at the chance to paint for cash, even if it wasn't much.

How can I say no to Aunt Clara? She couldn't, of course. Aunt Clara had been a source of stability in her life when her parents' marriage had fallen apart and her mother decided to move away from their tiny hometown to the much larger metro. She couldn't deny her aunt this favor, even if painting an entire mural would take a few weeks. Madeleine groaned as she cradled her head in her hands. She had to do it. She had to take the job.

Slowly, painstakingly, Madeleine typed out a reply accepting the offer, although she made sure to sound as reluctant as possible. She wanted Aunt Clara to know this wasn't a task she'd be taking on lightly. And she didn't want to give any sort of impression that she might be changing her mind about God and the church any time soon.

Before she sent the message, Madeleine paused one last time. A whole summer in Shady Springs, Arkansas? With Aunt Clara's church? The same congregation that had abandoned her mother and her when they most needed help?

I'm delaying the inevitable. Madeleine knew, no matter what, she would accept her aunt's proposal, and dragging out her response would not change things one bit. Maybe it wouldn't be so bad. It had been ten years since she left Shady Springs. A lot could change in ten years.

In a moment of bravery—or stupidity—before she could rethink her choice, Madeleine clicked SEND. It's too late now. The email is out there in space, making its way over to Aunt Clara.

Madeleine reclined in her chair and expelled a big breath. Another glance at her inbox revealed an even more disturbing sight. Is that who I think it is? How did he even get my email address? She opened the message and scanned its contents. She quickly deleted it and then emptied the trash folder.

Hands shaking, Madeleine closed her laptop. Why was it that on this particular morning, her past was determined to haunt her? What kind of summer had Madeleine signed up for?

* * *

"Need me to put those away?" A.J. Young poked his head into the classroom of his colleague, Clara Lewis. He was more than happy to lend a hand after Clara had helped him so many times.

"Thank you, A.J. I think I'll take you up on that offer."

Clara was surrounded by boxes of books and lab equipment. The sheen of sweat on her forehead and slightly glazed look in her eyes did little to diminish her inexhaustible spunk. Clara Lewis was small in stature but large in personality. Her blonde hair was always cut in a sensible but pretty style—short enough to not get in the way of a chemistry experiment, but long enough to still frame her face nicely. The few laugh lines around her mouth and eyes were marks of a joyful soul. Only one wrinkle, right between her eyebrows, gave a hint to the great pain Clara had suffered.

A.J. lifted everything onto the built-in shelf at the back of the room. "I can't believe your classroom is so clean and organized." He surveyed the empty space. With all of the happy chaos that usually filled the room, he'd never realized how big it actually was. "It must be time for summer!"

Clara sighed good-naturedly and leaned against one of the sturdy wooden tables. "Between end-of-the-year meetings, supply inventory, and packing my room, I'm ready for a break."

After teaching history and coaching track every day for two years,

A.J. couldn't imagine staying in this profession for another twenty. All he knew was that deep in his heart, he believed this was where God wanted him to be right now. Working with high school students was fulfilling and fun, and getting to learn from talented people like Clara Lewis made the job even better.

"Do you need me to stack those tables?" He pointed to Clara's hefty- looking perch.

Clara laughed. "Thank goodness, no. These things are a thousand pounds. I wouldn't be able to move them even if I had your help. The summer crew will take them out once it's time to wax the floor." Clara stood and dusted off her hands. "I think that about does it. I only have to turn in my paperwork, then it's summertime and easy living for me. How about you?"

"I've turned everything in already, but I'm sticking around a couple weeks for summer school and working at the church building the rest of the time." Even during vacations, A.J. enjoyed staying busy. Mowing lawns and mopping floors didn't require any lesson planning or mental strain from him and were a lot better than sitting around the house.

Clara's phone pinged.

"Ah! I've been waiting for an email ..." As Clara read her phone screen, her face transformed from expectant to concerned to elated. "She said yes! Oh, A.J.! My niece is coming to paint the church mural!"

"That's wonderful news, Clara! I'm sure it'll be nice for you to get to visit with her." A.J. knew from experience how lonely and long a summer break could be, and his heart lifted knowing Clara would have some company to keep her occupied.

"It will." Clara turned her attention to A.J. with a glint in her eyes. "She's single, you know. And she could use a good man."

A.J. took that as his cue to leave. "I'd better go." He chuckled nervously. "I'll see you later."

He'd already taken off down the hallway when he heard her call after him. "Wait! She's really special! I'll show you a picture!"

"Hey! Excuse me. This salad is still terrible."

Madeleine turned toward the direction of table nine, trying her best to keep a smile on her face. "I'm so sorry to hear that."

The salad was the second she'd returned, and the third plate overall for the rowdy group. Technically, they were at tables nine, ten, and six shoved together. Despite their "Sunday best" attire, they had all been on their worst behavior since the moment they walked into the restaurant, complaining about the music, the temperature, and the slow service. She just knew they would want their check split six or seven ways across all three tables.

"Do you see how wilted the lettuce is?" The lady shoved her plate in Madeleine's face. "I can't eat this."

"Well, ma'am, the meat on the brisket salad is pretty hot, and sometimes the lettuce wilts a little from the heat. I promise you all of our food is very fresh."

The woman stared back with her lips pursed. "I'd like to see your manager."

Madeleine sighed and nodded. "Of course. I'll go get her

right away." She turned and walked to the kitchen, breathing deeply and counting to ten.

"Staci. It's table nine. I can't make them happy no matter what I do." She rubbed her temples. "I hate Sundays so much."

"Me too, sweetie. I'll see what I can do." Staci patted her on the shoulder and marched off to do battle.

Madeleine grabbed a pitcher of water and made the rounds to her other tables. She hated how a difficult customer always sucked up all her attention and threw off her rhythm. Normally, she was a great waitress, but on days like today, she couldn't perform her best and would be better off curled up in a ball at home.

Staci returned from table nine and gave Madeleine a small smile. "I comped the salad and gave them a free ice cream." She typed on the cash register.

"Seriously, Stace? Now they'll be around an extra half hour." Madeleine groaned.

"I know. It was the only thing that would get them to stop complaining." Staci grimaced apologetically.

"I guess I should go take their order again." Madeleine started toward the table.

"No need. I got it already. You just worry about your other tables right now." A receipt printed from the register, and Staci ripped it off.

Madeleine sighed in relief. "Thanks, Staci. I owe you one."

Staci barked a laugh. "One? You owe me at least a hundred, girl."

"True." Madeleine grinned now. "How can I ever repay you?"

"Maybe you could start by staying in town instead of heading off to Arkansas this summer." Staci cocked her head and lifted her eyebrows.

"I wish I could … it's not that easy. I owe my aunt about a

million more favors than I owe you." She headed off to her other customers.

After another two tables had come and gone, the busboy was finally able to clean off tables nine, ten, and six and return them to their proper places. Madeleine shouldn't get her hopes up for a big tip, but her heart sank when she saw what they'd left.

"It's a Bible tract." Madeleine slammed the pamphlet down on the counter by the cash register.

Staci sighed and shook her head. "I'm so sorry. It's always the worst ones who do that."

"I wasn't expecting much, but I thought they'd at least give me something." She growled. "It's like they come in here just to make us feel small."

"They do a great job of it, too." Staci shook her head.

"I know there are decent Christians out there, like my Aunt Clara."

"And my grandparents." Staci pointed a finger at Madeleine.

"But the people we serve on Sunday afternoons don't make anyone actually want to be a Christian."

"Amen, sister. I don't want to spend any more time with Christians after working lunch today." She held up her hands as she marched off with the receipt.

Madeleine sighed. She didn't particularly want to spend any more time with Christians, either. She knew there were good ones out in the world, but she always seemed to end up with the bad apples. Especially in Shady Springs. So why had she agreed to spend an entire summer with them?

* * *

"There's something I want to talk to you about." Madeleine set the glasses on the tiny wooden table in the eat-in kitchen of the small house she shared with her mother, Catherine Mullins. "Aunt Clara asked me to stay with her for the summer."

"Oh?" Madeleine's mother didn't lift her gaze from tossing a big Greek salad for their dinner. After that afternoon's terrible customers, Madeleine hadn't wanted to see another salad for a long time. But she could make an exception for her mother.

"Yeah. She has a project for me, and I figured it's a good time, since I just finished the job for the hospital." Madeleine paused to gauge her mother's reaction to the news. "Plus, I could hardly tell Aunt Clara no."

"What's the project?" Her mom finally made eye contact as she moved the salad to the table, and the pleasant expression on her face encouraged Madeleine to continue.

"A mural."

"For her house?"

"No, for the church."

Catherine froze with her back turned as she reached for plates in the cupboard. Madeleine waited an eternity for her mother to face her again.

"I see."

"Listen, I already accepted, so it would be difficult to back out now, but if you really don't want me to do it, I don't have to." Madeleine chewed on her lip.

Catherine sighed. "If you already accepted, I suppose it would be rude to turn her down at this point."

"Right. I don't want to be rude."

"You're a grown woman now ... I just don't want you to get hurt.

Again."

Madeleine's defensive armor melted, and she had nothing but sympathy in her heart for her mother. She was torn between obligation to her mom and affection for her aunt, not to mention her integrity as a professional who had given her word.

She gazed into the eyes of the woman who had been her only parent for over a decade. Her mom's dark eyes and golden-brown hair were just the beginning of the similarities between them. The same sense of loyalty and sensitivity that could land her mother in trouble or tears ran deep in Madeleine's veins. Coupled with the intense aversion to conflict they also shared, she could completely understand where this concern was coming from.

"I know, Mom. I'll be careful." She placed a hand on her mother's shoulder. "It's only a job."

"Sure, sweetie." Madeleine's mom kissed her on the forehead and sat to eat.

Madeleine's happiness at having won this particular battle faded as she realized her biggest challenges were still ahead of her, waiting in Shady Springs.

Madeleine hadn't been to Shady Springs in a while, but the four-hour drive was as beautiful as Madeleine remembered. Dense emerald forests gave way to rolling hills covered in trees stretching as far as the eye could see. A thick, sultry June air wafted through the window, heavy with the scents of rain and earth.

She exited the interstate and drove through miles of country highways bordered by bright green meadows dotted with grazing cattle, brown and black. As she came into town, Madeleine took a detour and slowed in front of Clara's church building—the last church she had ever really been a part of.

The structure had grown since she was a child, and likely the number of members had grown as well, but the same red brick and long, rectangular windows faced out toward the highway. A sign out front read, "God loves you and we do too." Madeleine barked a laugh at that. If she and her mother had been shown real love, they never would have left the church, never would have left Shady Springs. She took a deep breath and sped past the building. This was going to be harder than she thought.

Clara's house was a renovated, two-story Colonial about halfway between the church building and the high school. The house had buttercream yellow siding, bright white trim, and a bold crimson front door. Unpainted wooden shutters and cheery flower boxes overflowing with begonias framed each window. Beds of hostas and ferns ringed two tall maple trees in the front yard.

As Madeleine pulled in front of the two-car detached garage, Clara ran to meet her. The dirt stains on the knees of her aunt's capri pants and the glimmer of sweat on her brow showed she'd been working in the garden this evening. In spite of her disheveled appearance, she exuded happiness. Aunt Clara was always most beautiful in summer. Her short blonde hair bleached by the sun, her skin bronzed despite frequent applications of sunscreen, and her schedule wide open to receive guests and grow all kinds of delicious herbs and vegetables.

"Oh, I'm so happy you're here!" Clara wrapped Madeleine in a hug. "Let me get your bags."

Madeleine was swept away by her aunt's bubbly enthusiasm, which was always a little overwhelming after living with her quiet, cautious mother for so long. The two sisters were five years apart in age but light years apart in personality. Where Catherine was steady and even- keeled, Clara was spontaneous and wild. She'd calmed some over the years, especially since Uncle George passed away from cancer—it would be exactly four years and two months this week if her math was correct. In the past, Uncle George would have closely followed Aunt Clara in the race to Madeleine's car. A surrogate father to her after her own father left, Madeleine's uncle had always provided a shoulder to cry on or sound advice in times of need. Although she could quickly call to memory the exact day he died, the exact dress she wore to his funeral, sometimes she would forget he was gone, only to be reminded and feel her heart clench again at the loss.

Before Madeleine could stop her, Aunt Clara hefted one of Madeleine's heavy bags onto her shoulder, pointing to the garden as she walked. "I was just checking on my tomatoes. They're going to be gorgeous this year. I can feel it. Hopefully, you'll get to have some. I don't know how long these murals normally take to finish."

"I'll have to look at the space and figure out the design, but it will probably take a few weeks." They'd emailed back and forth about the project, but Madeleine still didn't have many details to go off of. She was itching to get to work. The quicker the better, in Madeleine's opinion. If she worked fast enough, those tomatoes would still be tiny green babies by the time she left.

"Perfect!" Clara grinned. "I'm so happy you agreed to come. It'll be nice to have you here. Do you think your mom might come for a visit?"

"Probably not." Madeleine hadn't talked about that possibility with her mother, but she was unlikely to come given her reaction to Madeleine taking the job. With her new commission, avoiding church activities and church members would be nearly impossible. "She has a really busy schedule right now." True, but not the main reason for her absence. Madeleine suspected Aunt Clara knew the real cause.

"Well, maybe we can convince her to change her mind." Clara winked.

Madeleine unpacked her bags upstairs and texted her mother to let her know she'd arrived safely. After a delicious meal of chicken kabobs and rice pilaf, Madeleine and her aunt settled down with coffee and banana pudding in the living room.

"Mmm. Mom never lets us have dessert." Madeleine closed her eyes contentedly and savored the sweet, creamy dish.

"Everything in moderation, I always say." Clara licked her spoon. "Mom hasn't listened to that advice." Madeleine frowned a little.

"She can be pretty rigid about health food."

"She can be pretty rigid about a lot of things." Clara grimaced. "I'm sorry, I didn't mean—"

"No, you're right." Madeleine set her empty bowl on the side table.

"I know you and your mother are close, especially since your father left." Aunt Clara's eyes were kind and prompted Madeleine to continue, despite the emotional baggage surrounding the memories of her father.

"She's my best friend. And I love her." Madeleine paused to weigh her words carefully. "But I worry she doesn't have enough friends her own age. She hardly ever gets out and has fun."

"Her job at the hospital keeps her busy."

"That's part of it," Madeleine said. "But she stays in on her days off or only hangs out with me. I'm worried that after … after what happened at church …"

"She's too afraid to open up again?" Clara shifted, leaning forward. Madeleine nodded. She fiddled with a piece of string on the couch.

Finally, she decided to ask the question weighing on her mind. How long would it be before she had to confront Nancy Jones?

"Is she still here?" Madeleine maintained her focus on the couch, her gaze lowered.

"Who?" Clara cocked her head.

"You know … the woman who …" Madeleine waved her hands in the air, struggling to form the words.

"Oh! Nancy?"

Madeleine winced at the name. "Yeah."

"She's still here … You know, she's really sorry about what happened.

With your mom."

"Did she tell you that?" Madeleine had a hard time believing such a mean-spirited woman would go out of her way to apologize.

14

"No, but I think she would if I asked." Aunt Clara was always quick to believe the best in people, even if they didn't deserve it.

"How do you know?" Madeleine threw her arms up in exasperation. "I just do." Clara's voice was calm, though the wrinkle between her brows deepened.

"That might be enough for you to forgive her, but it's not good enough for me." Madeleine rose. "Thank you for dinner. I'd better get ready for bed now." She hated to end the evening on such a sour note, but she was afraid things would get even worse if she stuck around.

"Wait." Aunt Clara caught her by the arm. "I made an early lunch appointment for you tomorrow with Sam."

"Sam?"

"Our preacher. He's really the one with the vision for this mural. I thought it'd be good for you two to meet straight away."

"Oh, right. Thanks for setting that up." Madeleine remembered his name from their emails. She usually preferred to arrange her own business meetings, but Aunt Clara was a couple steps ahead of her. She'd better make a good first impression at this lunch tomorrow if she was to appear at all professional.

"Good night, sweetie." Aunt Clara's voice was soft and full of love. "Night, Aunt Clara." Madeleine patted her aunt on the shoulder before turning toward the hall.

Madeleine walked upstairs to the front guest room to get ready for bed. The space was light but cozy. A blue and pink floral quilt covered the small bed in the middle of the room, and matching navy drapes framed a large window. Madeleine knew from experience that the window let in a lot of light in the morning, so although the sky had shifted to a dark indigo and fireflies danced across the front yard, she closed the blinds and curtains tightly. Morning sun was lovely for drawing and painting, not so great for sleeping.

A heavy pit settled in Madeleine's stomach. Nothing had

changed in this small town. We moved away, separated ourselves from these people, and yet I am instantly taken back to a decade ago. Years have passed, and I'm still stuck with the same old problems. What do I have to do to move past this hurt?

Well, some things had changed. For starters, Shady Springs had a new preacher. As she pulled on her pajamas, Madeleine wondered about Sam. If she'd never heard of him before Aunt Clara's email, he must be a recent transplant, and that could work in her favor. A fresh face, unjaded and ignorant of Madeleine's past might be exactly what she needed to get through this summer. Maybe tomorrow would go really well. Maybe she'd finish the job quickly and return to life as usual. She could always hope.

* * *

The last day of kindergarten was over, and Maddy sat on the curb in front of school waiting for Daddy. He'd promised to take her for an ice cream cone to celebrate summer and finishing her first year of school. As she watched her friends' parents pick them up one by one, Maddy wondered if her mother hadn't been right. Maybe he would forget to get her.

They'd argued about that after dinner the night before. Daddy insisting he would remember; Mommy worried he wouldn't. In the end, Daddy had won, asking Mommy to please give him a chance. And now Maddy sat alone on the sidewalk outside the empty school building, a manila folder full of art and worksheets in her lap.

But then, as the last of her friends left from the car rider line, Maddy's father drove up in his rickety old red sedan. He rolled by slowly, one arm resting out the driver's side window, steering the car with a few fingers, and the other waving at her to get in the car.

"Hey, Maddy-Maddy-bo-Baddy! Hop in!"

"Hey, Daddy-Daddy-bo-Baddy!" Maddy leaped from the sidewalk with her folder and pulled open the back door. She fastened the seat belt as fast as she could and waved enthusiastically to the supervising teacher who appeared rather relieved to be sending off the last child.

"You're late, Henry." Miss Biel frowned. "I almost had to call Catherine to come pick her up."

Daddy flashed his toothy smile, the one that made women of every age forgive him immediately. "Sorry, Misty. I got busy with work. I know you teachers deserve a break after putting up with those snotty kids all year." At this, he turned and winked at Maddy. She winked back, just like she'd practiced in the mirror.

"Maddy's been talking about going to get ice cream all day. You better be good to that girl. She deserves a reward for all her hard work." Miss Biel was less irritated this time. No one could stay mad at Daddy very long.

"Oh, we're going to get ice cream all right. Aren't we, Maddy?"

"Three scoops!" Maddy called out.

"With chocolate!" Daddy turned and grinned at her. "And whipped cream!" Maddy shrieked.

"And cherries!" Daddy crowed.

"All right, you get outta here." Miss Biel smiled now. "Have a good summer, Maddy. See you later, Henry."

Daddy waved to Miss Biel as they sped out of the elementary school parking lot and onto the residential roads that surrounded the school.

"How was your last day of kindergarten? Did you learn everything you need to know?"

"We didn't really learn anything today. We did get an extra recess, though.

But Cody Owens wouldn't let me play with him."

"What? Why?" Daddy whipped his head around for a

second. "Because I'm a girl. And also, he said my freckles are dumb."

"He said what?" Now Daddy sounded sharp, almost angry.

"I have too many freckles, and they're dumb." She hated repeating what Cody had told her, except Daddy would be able to make it right. He always could.

"Sweetheart, if Cody is anything like his father, he will end up bald by the time he's in his twenties." Daddy sighed and put the car in park. He turned to Maddy straight on. "You listen good, Madeleine Jane Mullins. You and your mother are the two most beautiful women in the world, and nothing anyone says will ever change that. It doesn't matter what Cody Owens or anyone else thinks. You remember that, Maddy."

Maddy nodded with as serious a face as she could muster. What Cody had said hurt her at the time, but she hadn't cried. Cody would have made fun of her even more if she had. And she didn't tattle. What would the teachers even do to him on the last day of school? She just did what Mommy always told her to do and found someone else who needed a friend. Samantha Brown usually played alone on the swings, so Maddy decided to swing with her for the rest of the extra recess.

"I'll remember."

"Good girl. Now, who wants some ice cream?" His face broke into a smile. "Me! Me, me, me! But come help me with the seatbelt!" Maddy loved Daddy's beat-up car, but she could never push the old buckle quite hard enough to get herself out. Daddy came around to open her door and gave a sweeping, low bow.

"After you, mademoiselle."

"Merci!" Maddy had learned a few words in Spanish and French at school and liked to sprinkle them into conversation whenever possible. It definitely made her sound more grown-up and sophisticated.

After they'd finished their ice cream, Maddy showed her dad some of her artwork she'd brought home from school.

"This one was on the wall in the hallway. It's a drawing of a flower."

"Wow, Maddy! This is really good!"

"Do you like it?" Maddy was proud of the flower, but it meant so much more that Daddy liked it. He was a real artist.

"I love it!" Daddy glanced up from the drawing and beamed at her. "I love how you used color here. The way you drew with red and yellow and orange. It makes the flower seem almost like it's alive."

"Well … you can have it if you want it." She really loved the flower picture, but she wanted so badly to make Daddy happy.

"I do want it, Maddy, but you don't have to give it to me."

"I … I want you to have it," Maddy said. She knew it was the right thing to do, even if it made her heart hurt a little to think about giving up the picture.

"How about this? How about I keep it for you until you get bigger? I can hang it up in my studio."

"Okay!" That was a much better idea. Then she could see the picture anytime she wanted.

They walked down the street to his photography studio. Maddy went straight to the stack of new pictures that had been printed. Some were in black and white, but Maddy's favorites had lots of color. Daddy found a frame for the picture and hung it on the wall in the front waiting area.

"Oh, I guess lots of people will see it, won't they?"

"They will. Is that okay?" Daddy raised an eyebrow.

"Yeah." The thought of lots of people seeing her flower pleased Maddy. If Daddy liked it so much, maybe other people would enjoy seeing it, too. "You know what, Daddy?"

"What, Maddy-Maddy-Bo-Baddy?"

"I think I want to be an artist. Just like you."

Daddy knelt down. His gaze met hers. "I think you would make a very good artist. Even better than me."

"No one's better than you, Daddy."

*a*fter breakfast and a morning jog, Madeleine left to scope out the spot for the mural. Clara had given her a key to the church building to keep while she worked on the project, so she packed her tape measure and a notebook into her car and drove four blocks to the back parking lot of the building. Admittedly, driving such a short distance was a little silly, but Madeleine was meeting the preacher soon and didn't want to show up sweaty, rumpled, and frizzy from the humid summer air.

The hallway was dark and quiet when Madeleine unlocked the door, and her eyes adjusted slowly. As her vision cleared, Madeleine spotted a collage of pictures on a bulletin board. They showed smiling families eating at a picnic, playing silly games, and decorating cookies together. The congregation sure has grown since I was here last. Madeleine couldn't remember having many friends her age from church in Shady Springs. They certainly hadn't had any fun, family-oriented activities. Maybe things have changed more than I thought.

One photo in particular stood out. A group of kids and their parents posed and grinned with their arms around each other. They looked genuinely happy to be together. Madeleine couldn't help but smile, too, and she turned the hall corner a little lighter on her feet. She'd accepted this job out of love for Aunt Clara, but now that she'd seen the faces of the children for whom she would be painting, she had a connection with the project she'd been missing before. Something about their smiles reminded Madeleine of happier times at the Shady Springs church. Vacation Bible School, singing at the local nursing home, her Sunday Bible classes—not every memory of this congregation was bad.

Madeleine roamed the halls, searching for her mural space. Enough dim light flowed in through the windows that she could barely make her way around, but this wing was new, and her faded mental map of the building was not helpful. Finally, she found a large, blank space on the wall outside the "Family Life Center" with a sign reading "Coming Soon!!! A mural by famous artist Madeleine Mullins!"

Madeleine rolled her eyes and chuckled as she flipped on the nearby light switch. This sign reeked of Aunt Clara.

She took the tape measure out of her pocket and began recording the length and height of the space, then drew a few rough sketches of the hallway, including doors, outlets, and anything else pertinent to her work. She also pulled out her phone—almost as good as her DSLR camera—to take some pictures of the wall. She hadn't realized how quiet the building was until she heard a noise.

Slam!

Madeleine jumped and fumbled to catch her pencil and notebook. Was the sound just a church member slamming the front door? Maybe Sam had come to meet her here instead of the restaurant. Or was it someone more nefarious?

"Hello?" Madeleine called out timidly. Silence. Perhaps she could yell a little louder. "Hello! Who's there?"

Silence again. Maybe she'd imagined the noise, and no one was there after all.

Thump.

Nope, definitely someone there. She would have to investigate.

Madeleine opened the nearest door to find something to use as protection, just in case. The room appeared to be a children's classroom, and they must have been studying the Armor of God because Madeleine found a long, wooden sword labeled "Spirit" at the front of the room. Brandishing the weapon in one hand and her phone in the other, Madeleine reentered the hallway.

Thud.

She followed the source of the noises until she was fairly certain she was around the corner from the intruder. Madeleine took a deep breath and jumped into the hallway, crashing into a tall man and accidentally whacking him with the sword in the process, landing on her rear end.

She scrambled backward. Looked up. Felt completely ridiculous because the auburn-haired guy—young, handsome guy—was wearing earbuds and carrying a phone. And nothing about him suggested mal- intent. In fact, a bright yellow bucket spinning down the hallway suggested he was actually here to mop the floors.

"I'm so sorry!"

"Who are you?" His voice was shocked but not harsh.

Madeleine's cheeks burned. "Madeleine. I'm so sorry! I called out, but no one answered, so I thought—but of course you were wearing headphones, or you would have heard me—and obviously you work here, since, you know, you have a mop—" Shut up! Stop talking! She clamped her mouth closed to prevent any more words from leaking out. The young man stared at her, dumbfounded, and for a moment, Madeleine wished she could sink into the floor. Turn into a puddle he could mop up.

But then he smiled. And it was the most handsome grin she had ever seen. Her stomach filled with butterflies as he burst into laughter.

"Is that a sword from the props bin?"

"Yeah, I …" Madeleine's embarrassment fizzled away as relief that the young man wasn't an angry intruder—and wasn't upset with her—washed over her.

"I'm A.J." He offered a hand to help her up from the floor. "You must be Clara Lewis's niece."

"Guilty." In more ways than one.

Madeleine took his hand, noticing how strong and calloused it was.

He pulled her up easily, making her forget her embarrassment for a moment.

A.J. had the build of someone who was used to hard work, but his easy smile and teasing eyes told her he had a fun-loving streak a mile wide.

"Famous artist, Madeleine Mullins in the flesh. How could I be so lucky?" He looked genuinely pleased to meet her, despite the fact that she'd attacked him only moments before.

Madeleine's heart skipped a beat as he flashed another smile.

"You've seen the sign, I presume?" She guessed that was how he knew her name.

"Oh, sure. It's all Clara has been able to talk about ever since you agreed to come."

"She's a very proud aunt." Although I wish she would turn the pride down a notch.

"And a dedicated matchmaker." A.J. produced a photo from his pocket—a wallet-sized picture of Madeleine, something Clara had probably printed from her social media profile. Madeleine's face must be a bright vermillion by now. Could she possibly humiliate herself even more?

"I don't know what to say. I can't believe she did this. I'm sorry."

A.J. grinned. "She thinks very highly of you."

"Perhaps a little too highly." Madeleine would have words with her aunt when she got home.

"We'll see." A.J.'s mouth turned up at the corner. "I assume I'll be seeing a lot of you this summer. I come in to clean and mow and do some general maintenance."

Madeleine liked the idea of seeing more of A.J., but she didn't want their first meeting to be exactly how all their encounters would unfold. "If that's the case, maybe we should establish some ground rules."

A.J. raised his eyebrows.

"For example," Madeleine said, "you could call out before you come into the building. That way I don't accidentally hit you. Again."

"Sounds reasonable enough." A.J.'s face fell into its previous mischievous smile. "And perhaps you could be a little more careful when wielding dangerous weapons."

"Deal." Madeleine grinned back. "I hope I didn't hurt you too badly."

"No." A.J. lifted his sleeve and inspected his shoulder. "Only a flesh wound."

"Good." Madeleine checked the time on her phone. "I should probably pack my things. I'm supposed to meet Sam in a little while to talk about the mural."

"Well, Madeleine Mullins, famous artist, I hope we do not meet like this again."

"I agree, A.J. Next time, no weapons and no surprises."

"Deal." A.J. stuck out his hand to shake.

Madeleine shook his hand and returned his smile. She regretted meeting A.J. the way she had. And she was horrified that Clara had been passing around her picture. She hoped not too many other guys had gotten the hard sell from Aunt Clara. In fact, she hoped A.J. was the only one.

* * *

What just happened?

A.J.'s head was still spinning from his brief interaction with Madeleine Mullins. He'd known she was pretty from the picture Clara gave him. Why had he even kept that thing? Madeleine must think he was a creep for carrying around a photo of her in his wallet, although the expression on her face had been priceless.

A.J. shook his head, turning to retrieve his cleaning supplies. He chuckled as he walked down the hall. The young woman definitely knew how to make an impression.

As he rolled the mop bucket over to the sink to fill it with water and soap, he remembered what Clara had shared about Madeleine. He knew she was an artist and that she wasn't a Christian. He knew she used to live in Shady Springs and now lived in Kansas City with her mom. It really wasn't much to go off. And the little information he had hadn't been enough to prepare him for his … encounter … with Madeleine.

This wasn't the first time A.J. had witnessed the infamous matchmaking of Clara Lewis, but it was the first time he'd been on the receiving end. Resisting Clara had been a lot easier when he'd never actually met Madeleine. Now he knew she had a fiery personality to match her incredibly good looks. But a romance wasn't meant to be.

A.J. would certainly try to be nice to the girl, but he couldn't see anything more than friendship happening between them. Madeleine wasn't a Christian, and faith was the most important thing in his life.

He'd been going to church as long as he could remember, and he'd always loved leading prayers or preaching sermons. But the moment that A.J.'s life changed had actually been years after he became a Christian, the summer before he went to college.

A.J.'s church had just hired a new youth minister who worked very hard all year to make sure his teens knew their scripture well. And then he worked even harder to give them a week at church camp they'd never forget. Every day they studied the book of Romans and what it had to say about God's love. On the last night, each student wrote down sins they struggled with on a shoe box and built a wall at the end of a large pavilion. After a rousing sermon and moving song service, the youth minister read from Romans 8:38-39 "For I am sure that neither death nor life, nor angels nor rulers, nor things present nor things to come, nor powers, nor height nor depth, nor anything else in all creation, will be able to separate us from the love of God in Christ Jesus our Lord."

As he read the verses, a wooden cross swung down and knocked over all of the boxes covered with their sins. A.J. had known but never truly internalized that God had forgiven him once and for all. And nothing in the world would stand between Him and His children. At that moment, A.J. decided he would do his best to never let anything come before God. And a couple years later, he decided he really wanted to work with kids, just like that youth minister.

A.J. lifted the mop. A twinge pulled at his shoulder. Maybe he wouldn't be anything more than friends with Madeleine, but he couldn't deny she'd made a lasting impression. His shoulder certainly wouldn't let him forget her quickly.

At the very least, A.J. wanted to share with Madeleine what his youth minister had shared with him. God wanted a relationship with her more than anything in creation, and Jesus had died to make it possible.

Whether or not A.J. would be able to become good friends with Madeleine, he hoped he had a chance to see her again soon.

4

*M*adeleine pulled up to the sandwich shop at noon and saw a man waiting inside who must be Sam. He

appeared to be in his mid-forties with a full head of salt and pepper hair—mostly pepper. As she walked into the restaurant, he lifted his head and smiled kindly. If the wrinkles on his face were any indication, Sam smiled a lot.

"You must be Madeleine." He rose and shook her hand vigorously. "I'm Samuel Sullivan. You can call me Sam."

"Nice to meet you, Sam." Madeleine couldn't help but return his warm grin.

"I waited on you to order. I'll pick up the tab since this is a working lunch."

They moved to the counter and placed orders for two sandwich meals. Madeleine glanced around the restaurant. The walls were painted a bright yellow and covered with artwork. On closer inspection, each piece wore a price tag. Underneath the paintings and photographs were names of local artists. Most of the art was … a bit amateurish, but one or two paintings were really nice. Madeleine might consider buying them if she had any money to spare.

"Everything here comes with a warm, chocolate chip cookie. If you don't care for them, I'd be happy to help you finish yours." Sam winked at her good-naturedly.

"Oh, I think I can handle it. Thanks for the offer." Madeleine chuckled.

They sat with their drinks and waited for their lunch. Small, wooden tables and chairs were crammed together at the front of the restaurant. Sam chose a spot with a great view of the street outside. The tables were all brightly painted with flowers and trees and birds. Madeleine's chair had stars on a midnight blue background; Sam's was covered in fluffy clouds.

"So, Madeleine, tell me about yourself. Why did you choose to study art?"

"I've always loved drawing and creating." Madeleine smiled. "I used to drive Mom crazy with the random stuff I would collect to turn into sculptures. And I always had paint or ink on my hands. She called me Sticky Fingers. Or Mad Madeleine, because I looked like a mad scientist with my hair all frizzy and my clothes a mess.

"I fell in love with painting—murals specifically—during a workshop my freshman year of college. I got a couple jobs in the summers and then a really big job for the children's hospital. And here I am today."

The cashier came by with their sandwiches and two chocolate chip cookies. "Here you go, Sam. Enjoy."

"Thanks, Jessica."

Madeleine took a tiny bite of her soft, still-warm cookie. It was amazing.

"Mmm. If the sandwiches are this good, I can see why you come here." Madeleine inspected her turkey, bacon, and avocado on sourdough approvingly before digging in. "So, what about you, Sam?" She washed down her food with a sip of sweet tea. "Why did you decide to become a preacher?"

"Well ... That's a long story, but I can give you the short version. I was raised in the foster system and met some good people along the way. A lot of bad people, mind you, but God's hand was definitely guiding me— pulling me—toward Him.

"I ended up going to a Christian college on scholarship and getting baptized while I was there. I fell in love with Jesus and His church and realized I couldn't see myself doing anything else. I've been preaching in Shady Springs for five years now, and I think the Lord is doing wonderful things through the church here."

As he spoke, Madeleine could see there was definitely much more to this story. A shadow of sadness passed over his face as Sam talked about his early years, but there was a glint of hope and joy in his eyes as he shared his journey. He obviously loved God and was happy with his life in Shady Springs.

Sam set a hefty Bible on the table. If the cafe tables hadn't been recently cleaned, Madeleine could imagine a cloud of dust rising around them. This must be a Bible for only the most serious of Christians.

"Do you own one of these?"

"Not quite so large," Madeleine said. "I'm sure I have a much smaller one lying around the house somewhere. It's been a while since I read a Bible. Is that going to be a problem?"

"I'd like you to try again. Just for this project. And just one book." Sam flipped through the pages.

"Which book?" She hadn't anticipated a homework assignment attached to this commission.

"The Gospel according to Matthew." Sam pointed to the beginning of Matthew and turned the Bible around to face Madeleine. "I think it best captures the message I'd like to convey in the mural."

"And what message is that exactly?" Madeleine asked apprehensively.

Perhaps she hadn't really thought this project through.

"I want the mural to be less about showing a picture of the face of Jesus and more about showing how He touched the lives of those around Him. The miracles, the lessons, the ways He changed people. We don't need to know what Jesus looked like to follow Him. We do need to be reminded of His love." There was that glint again. Sam must really love Jesus to get so excited about Him.

"And you think I need to read Matthew in order to paint that?"

Madeleine raised an eyebrow. This was turning into more of a sermon than she'd signed up for.

"Yes. You seem like an intelligent girl. It won't take you very long at all. You may even decide you want to read a little bit more." Sam gave another of his contagious smiles.

"Sorry to disappoint you, but I don't think that's very likely." She'd had quite enough of church and the Bible. And she didn't want to get Sam's hopes up thinking this mural would have some fairy tale happy ending. This commission was only a job, nothing more.

"Well, either way, Matthew is a good place to start. You know, it was written by a tax collector."

This was probably a trap to get her asking questions about the Bible, but Sam had piqued her curiosity. "Like the IRS?"

"Sort of." Sam appeared satisfied she'd taken the bait. "He was a Jew, but he worked for the occupying government. Other Jews were not a big fan of tax collectors. They were seen as traitors. Jesus was not very popular for His habit of spending time with tax collectors."

"So why did He do it?" Madeleine mentally chided herself for asking another question. This guy was good.

"Simple. He loved them. Jesus said himself, 'It is not the

healthy who need a doctor, but the sick.' We're all sinners. We can't always see that in ourselves, but God sees us as we are. Everyone needs forgiveness."

Sam paused and pursed his lips. Madeleine tried to arrange her face into an interested expression, but she worried Sam noticed her attention beginning to wane.

"I'll let you digest that little sermon, and we can pick up again later." He patted the Bible on the table. "You take this one home with you. I have more than enough to spare."

As Sam rose to throw away their trash, Madeleine flipped through the pages of the massive book. The feel of the onion-skin pages, smooth and thin, brought back memories, and a longing washed over her. What would her life be like if she'd never left the church?

Sam returned, and the memories vanished. He walked her out to the parking lot. "I hope to see you at the ice cream social tomorrow night.

I'll be making my famous browned butter pecan." Sam wiggled his eyebrows.

"That sounds delicious, but I might be busy." No way was she going to start attending church social events. Even if there was ice cream on the line.

"Don't worry. Everyone at church is mostly normal." He laughed. "We don't bite. At least, as long as there's ice cream."

Right. I'd have to disagree with that assessment.

"I assume Aunt Clara will be there, so I might not have a choice." Better to get Sam off her back than continue standing in the parking lot arguing with him.

"Wonderful! I'll see you there!" He waved and walked toward the crosswalk.

A burst of hot air flew out of the car as Madeleine opened the door. She reached in to take down the sun reflectors—a lot of good those did—before sinking into the warm seat and turning on the AC.

She pulled out of the parking lot and drove the five minutes it took to get through downtown Shady Springs and into her aunt's neighborhood. As she thought about her assignment from Sam and the time she'd have to spend with the church members, black dread wrapped around her lungs. A sensation of sinking into a pit of her own making threatened to overwhelm her. Fear—of being judged again and of being hurt again—was her constant companion on this trip.

"I'm back!" Madeleine called into the house when she returned. "Hellooo!"

Silence greeted her, and a quick investigation of the kitchen table revealed a note saying Clara had left to run some errands.

Too wound up to rest and needing to start on her project, Madeleine carried her supplies and the massive Bible up the stairs to her bedroom. The room had a small desk on which Madeleine set her sketch pad, some pencils, and an eraser. The Bible, she put on the bed to read later. Sometime.

Madeleine downloaded the photos from earlier in the day and fiddled around with them for a few minutes on her laptop. She glanced at the Bible on her bed.

Then she pulled out the sketches she'd drawn earlier and flipped to a blank page. Her gaze scanned the room and fell on the Bible again. She drew a few lines half-heartedly.

Fine.

If this were a normal project, she would have come into an initial meeting with renderings or at least a couple good ideas ready to go. She would certainly be willing to read something the client wanted her to use for inspiration. She shouldn't be so quick to dismiss Sam's request just because he was a preacher and the mural was for a church.

Madeleine plopped down on the bed and cracked open the Bible. The song she learned as a child popped into her head. Matthew, Mark, Luke and John ... Matthew was at the beginning of the New Testament. She'd always had more trouble with the

Old Testament. Now, where in the world do I find the New Testament in this tome? She flipped to the front index and then turned toward the Gospel according to Matthew. Now she could see why Sam's Bible was so thick. Only about half of each page contained actual Bible verses. The bottom portion of every page gave comments and cross-references and who-knew-what-else for the verses above. Maybe the weight of the book would prove to be useful as Madeleine hadn't read a Bible since childhood.

As she scanned through the first few verses—the family tree of Jesus—she got to some familiar passages. Madeleine remembered studying the birth of Jesus in Sunday school, and many verses stuck out as ones she'd read before. She read on through the baptism and temptation of Jesus, stopping a few times to check the notes at the bottom of the page before she heard Clara come in through the front door. Quickly, Madeleine shut the Bible, nervous to be caught doing the one thing Clara desperately wanted her to do. She couldn't stand the thought of disappointing her beloved aunt.

Madeleine reflected over what she'd read and what Sam had talked about at lunch. She'd decided a long time ago she believed in God, or at least some higher power. There was too much beauty and love in the world for it to be an accident, and having no higher being and no heaven—somewhere out there— meant that all of the sadness and pain in the world had no happy ending.

The truth was Madeleine hadn't given her faith much thought recently. She believed the evidence pointed to the God of the Bible, but she hadn't been able to stomach the thought of returning to a church building. And she was only twenty-two. She had plenty of life ahead of her. God was something she could figure out when she got a little older and a little wiser.

Madeleine sat up as she heard a knock at the door. "Come in!"

"Hey, sweetie. Wanted to let you know I'm home. I picked

some fresh basil today—thought we could have pesto for supper. Sound good?" Aunt Clara's happy face and the promise of pasta made Madeleine momentarily forget her deep thoughts.

"Sure, Aunt Clara. I'll come downstairs and help you in a minute."

Madeleine stared at the wall as she tried to clear her head of all the questions she still had. Maybe she should read a little more before coming to Aunt Clara or Sam with them. Maybe she needed to reexamine her beliefs.

5

The next morning, Madeleine joined Clara for a bowl of cereal and sliced fruit.

"We've got the church ice cream social tonight at the park. I'm going to need someone there to keep me from sampling every single flavor." Clara was mostly teasing, but her sweet tooth was legendary. Unfortunately, the love of everything sugary ran in the family, which could be why Madeleine's mom was always so careful to keep junk food out of the house.

"You know I wouldn't be much help in that area." Madeleine took a deep breath. Breakfast was too early in the morning for an argument, but she should be honest with her aunt. "I'm not sure I'm ready to throw myself to the wolves yet."

Clara's smile faded into a frown of concern. "It's been ten years, Madeleine. Don't you think it's time to give them a second chance?"

"Why do they deserve any chances?"

"None of us deserve another chance." Aunt Clara's voice was kind and calm, despite Madeleine's growing frustration. "That's the point. We've all messed up. 'For all have sinned and fallen short of the glory of God.'"

Clara sipped her coffee, and her brow wrinkled. "You don't have to talk to anyone you don't want to. And it's really the only way you'll get supper tonight, unless you want to cook something for yourself. Besides, it would be good to meet all the people who have hired you to paint their mural."

Madeleine was perfectly capable of cooking for herself, but Aunt Clara had a point. She probably should introduce herself to the people writing her check. She mentally weighed her options. Stay home and eat by herself or attend a church function with all of the church crowd and eat delicious ice cream.

"It's a close tie, but I guess I'll come along." Madeleine rose from the table and rinsed her plate.

"Great! I think you'll have a nice time."

"I hope so." She mumbled the words under her breath, doubtful of their truth.

Clara gave Madeleine a conspiratorial look over the top of her coffee mug.

"There might be some cute boys there, too."

"I don't need your help finding a boyfriend, Aunt Clara. Especially not one who lives four hours away from me." Madeleine rolled her eyes as she loaded her dishes in the dishwasher.

"You might change your mind, once you meet them."

"I already met one at the church building. A.J."

"Oh? What'd you think?" Aunt Clara raised her eyebrows.

"He was nice." Madeleine pursed her lips as she tried her best to keep a goofy grin off her face. "I'm not sure I made too good of an impression; although, he seemed to know quite a bit about me already. Know anything about that?"

"Hmm?" Clara was clearly pretending she hadn't given A.J. that picture of Madeleine.

"Like I said, I don't need you to find me a boyfriend. Stop handing out photos." She playfully swatted Aunt Clara's hand before heading upstairs to her bedroom.

Madeleine hadn't spoken with her mother in one whole day. Maybe a phone call would do her some good.

"Hey, Mom, how's it going?" Madeleine paced the room as she talked.

"Hi, sweetie!" In spite of her upbeat tone, Madeleine's mother sounded tired.

"Having a good day off work?"

"Yes, still recovering from yesterday." Catherine sighed. "I won't keep you long. I just wanted to check in."

"Have you started the painting yet?" Catherine asked. Was she asking this to make sure her daughter was behaving professionally or to make sure she was coming back home soon?

Madeleine glanced over at the mostly empty pages of her sketchbook. "I will soon … It's a little harder than I thought it would be, painting Jesus." She wasn't sure where to begin painting someone so important to so many people. Someone she hardly knew at all.

"Why is that?"

"I haven't read a Bible since I was a kid."

"You still are a kid."

"I know you think that, Mom, but I'm going to move out soon, and then I'll be on my own." Perhaps her mother would always think of her as a child. All the more reason to get her own place as soon as possible.

"Maybe this will be good for you. You should read the Bible again." She sipped a drink, almost certainly a cup of tea.

"What do you mean?"

"You know I never stopped believing in God." They'd traveled this path before. Madeleine was always a little reluctant to bring up the subject of faith, partly because of the painful memories that came with it and partly because she didn't have any real answers concerning God or religion. "I think you need to examine the evidence and decide for yourself what you believe."

But what if she sided with Aunt Clara? What if she decided following God meant going to church? What if following God required a level of commitment she simply wasn't ready for?

"I should let you get some rest. I'll check in again later." Madeleine wasn't sure where this conversation was headed and wanted it to end before things got too theological.

"Okay, sweetie. Love you."

That afternoon, Madeleine read a little more of Matthew. Sam had said he wanted to show how Jesus made people feel, and she tried to keep that in mind. As she dove into chapter 5, Jesus preached a sermon about how to act as a Christian that was really radical and, honestly, different from how most Christians —and most people—acted.

Love your enemies and pray for those who persecute you? Who actually does that?

The teachings of Jesus were impossible.

How can so many people claim to follow Jesus and not act this way?

After an afternoon of sketching Jesus preaching on the mountain and calling his disciples, Madeleine was shaken out of her concentration by a loud ringing. An unknown number flashed on the screen of her phone.

"Hello?"

"Madeleine? I can't believe it's really you."

Madeleine's heart raced. She couldn't be positive because it had been so long, but if she was right, she hadn't heard the voice on the other end for ten years. Panic stole the air from her lungs. A knot of crimson anger tightened right above her sternum. She pulled the phone from her ear and stared at the screen. Hung up. Deep breaths. Slowly, she set the phone on the nightstand.

How did he find me? First the email and now this phone call. Why now?

Madeleine lay on the bed and pulled the quilt around herself like a cocoon.

God, I don't know if You're listening, but I could use Your help.

$\mathcal{B}$y the time Madeleine woke, the sun had moved lower in the sky, casting a golden hue over her room, and the alarm clock on her nightstand read 5:30. The sounds of Clara moving around in the kitchen reminded her of the ice cream social in half an hour. She checked her appearance in the hall bathroom and decided a change of clothes was in order.

Madeleine didn't consider herself to be obsessed with clothing, but she could certainly appreciate a good outfit from an artistic point of view. She pulled on her favorite skirt—full with flamingos printed all over—and a black sleeveless top. Then she slid into her black espadrilles—both pretty and practical for an outdoor summer party—and added a couple bright pink and turquoise necklaces to finish it off.

"Wow, Maddy! You are completely right—you do not need my help getting a man," Clara teased when Madeleine came downstairs. She was packing tubs of blackberry fudge ice cream to take to the social.

"Listen, sweetie. I know you're coming as a favor to me, and I really appreciate it. Just try to make an effort and meet some new friends, okay?" Clara cupped Madeleine's chin in her hand, so she had no choice but to stare into her eyes. "I promise you'll be fine. It'll be a nice night.

The biggest danger is that I will almost certainly eat too much ice cream."

Madeleine laughed. They would both certainly eat too much ice cream.

Spring Park in Shady Springs was the center of the town, both literally and metaphorically. Within a couple acres of protected green space were pavilions, a playground, public restrooms, walking trails, and the regionally famous springs. Legend held that water from the springs had restorative properties. During the early days of Arkansas statehood, people had traveled from miles around to soak in the cool, tree-lined springs. In actuality, the water could not heal, unless the ailment happened to be a hot summer day.

Madeleine hadn't visited the park in many years and was delighted to find that not much had changed, except for the newly-updated restrooms. Church members had already laid out rows of ice cream makers and tubs filled with homemade creamy deliciousness. Someone had fired up a grill, and dozens of hot dogs filled an aluminum pan. Lawn chairs and metal folding chairs dotted the grass around the pavilion.

Madeleine panicked for a minute when Aunt Clara left her to set down the ice cream and started chatting with some older women. She was really not in the mood to talk to church ladies, so she grabbed a bottled water from one of the coolers on the pavilion floor and a hot dog from the table. Madeleine stood while eating her hot dog and scanned the crowd for a familiar face. She thought she could see A.J. with a group of teenagers, and without thinking, she started to walk toward him.

"The weather is supposed to be perfect, and the water level shouldn't be too high. If we can get a few more people to come, we'll be able to get the cost down a couple bucks." A.J. was facing away from Madeleine and addressing the cluster of kids around him.

"I'll have to ask off of work, but I think I should be able to tag along.

It sounds like fun." This was from a tall boy of about sixteen.

"Great! And ask Emma and Jessica if they'd like to join us. I put it in the bulletin, and I'll text everyone, but I've also posted a tentative schedule for the summer on the church website. Let me know if you think of anything you want to add." A.J. must be in charge of activities for the teens this summer.

"Sure, your schedule is wide open, teacher-man. Some of us have actual jobs in the summer." A second boy chuckled as he punched A.J. in the arm.

Despite the rib, Madeleine could tell he actually thought highly of

A.J. In fact, all the kids looked at him like they thought he'd hung the moon. They probably could've gone on talking a long time without noticing Madeleine's presence, but the first boy who spoke glanced up and saw her standing nearby. He smiled, and A.J. turned to see her.

"Madeleine Mullins in the flesh! Our resident artiste! Hey, everyone, this is Madeleine—Clara Lewis's niece. She's painting the mural in the new wing. Madeleine, this is Turner, Cooper, Mitchell, Sophie, and Caitlin. Don't bother learning names. I call them all 'hey you' most of the time."

Madeleine gave a small smile to each of them. A.J. was right. She probably wouldn't learn their names during her short time in Shady Springs. What was the point?

"That's so cool!" said a girl with dark hair and glasses. "Did you go to art school near here?"

"I went in Kansas City, so not too far away. That's where I live now."

"I love Kansas City. We went on a field trip to the Federal

Reserve last year and got to stay in a hotel and go to the mall."
The other girl was taller and blonde.

"We do have some great shopping. We also have really amazing barbecue."

"Yeah, Caitlin, try branching out a little." The blond boy laughed.

Caitlin's cheeks grew pink. "Well, I wasn't exactly in charge of the field trip."

"You should definitely come back sometime," Madeleine said in an attempt to smooth things over. "I'd love to show you around."

"Thanks." Caitlin smiled before lightly shoving the boy who had teased her.

Madeleine turned to face A.J. "Are you guys planning a trip?"

"We're going to canoe the Buffalo River on Monday. You should come with us!" His eyes lit up, excited.

"Oh, I didn't mean to—"

"I know, but if we get ten people to go, it will knock a few dollars off the price. It'll be a lot of fun, and the river is beautiful this time of year."

A.J. flashed what was no doubt intended to be a persuasive smile, and Madeleine's stomach flipped as she responded with a sappy grin.

She imagined peacefully floating down a river, just the two of them, the sun reflecting off his auburn hair. "I'll see if I can make time—"

"Great!" A.J. interrupted. His smile grew even bigger, and part of her was pleased to have made him happy, even if it had only been to get him a discount on his trip.

"—but only if I get lots of work done this weekend." This trip to Shady Springs was supposed to be a job, after all. Not frequent run-ins with a very handsome stranger.

"Sure, of course. We're meeting at the church building at

eight o'clock. Wear something you don't mind getting wet and water shoes if you have any. And bring a water bottle. Tell you what, how about I text you all the details?"

"Real smooth, A.J." Blond boy cracked up. "Now you have to get her phone number."

A.J. smiled and laughed along with the guys, but Madeleine could detect the hint of a blush on his cheeks.

"Is that okay?" he asked her, eyebrows raised.

"Of course." Madeleine reached for his cell phone and typed her number in his contacts. By the time she returned the phone, the teens had moved on to another topic of conversation. Something about class schedules or summer football practice.

"Do you hang out with high school students a lot?" she asked.

"Like it's my job!" A.J. chuckled. "It is, actually. My job, I mean. I teach with your aunt at the high school. And I coach. The church maintenance stuff is just a summer gig. I also help out with the youth group, unofficially. We try to plan at least one big activity a month—more during the summers."

"It's really great you help out so much. Teaching is such an important profession. I had an amazing art teacher in high school who helped me through some rough spots." Madeleine hoped she didn't sound too gushy. She held a soft spot in her heart for teachers. The weird part was, A.J. didn't sound stressed or resentful as he talked about all of his jobs. And after watching him interact with the teens, she sensed that he really loved what he did.

"Hey, why don't you have a bowl in your hands?" A.J. asked.

Madeleine lowered her gaze to the empty plate and water bottle she held. Must be time to get some ice cream.

"Come with me. I need a second helping anyway."

They walked through the line, and Madeleine filled a bowl with half a dozen small scoops, unable to decide on one flavor. A.J. stopped to say something to everyone he saw, which made getting their ice cream take twice as long. Madeleine perused the myriad flavors, sampling a little from her bowl while A.J. wasn't paying attention.

At one point, Madeleine saw Aunt Clara across the pavilion. She had an overly excited expression on her face. Madeleine quickly steered A.J. away before he could see Aunt Clara. "Let's go sit down before this all melts."

They found an empty picnic table near the pavilion.

"Had any more fencing practice lately?" A twinkle lit A.J.'s emerald eyes.

"No, I've missed my sparring partner." Did that sound weird? To say she missed him after such a short time? He'd certainly made a big impression, but she didn't need to let him know exactly how big.

"Well, maybe we can have a rematch someday." He shoveled a spoonful of strawberry ice cream into his mouth. "Mmm. I sure do love church potlucks."

"They are one of the best parts about church." Madeleine took a slightly more modest spoonful herself.

A.J. narrowed his eyes a bit, as if he were thinking about making a comment, but then the moment was over. "How's the mural coming?"

"Not bad. I'm still in the early stages. Sam's given me a reading assignment out of the massive book he calls his Bible."

"Ha." A.J. shook his head. "I bet Sam Sullivan has quite a few hefty Bibles. What does he have you reading?"

"Matthew." She shrugged. "I mean, I've read it all before, in bits and pieces as a kid. But he wants me to read it again for the mural."

A.J. nodded. "Hmm. Well, let me know if you need any help."

Madeleine raised an eyebrow. "You know, with all the money I spent on art school, they taught me how to paint and read."

He laughed and hit her lightly on the shoulder. "That's not what I meant. Just, if you have questions or whatever."

"Sure." Madeleine bent her head over her bowl, smiling to herself. "You seem to know a lot about me, I assume from my Aunt Clara, but I don't know anything about you. How long have you lived in Shady Springs?"

"How do you know I'm not a local?"

She cocked her head. "I'd know, trust me." She didn't have time to go into all the ways he stood out like a sore thumb among the rural Shady Springs crowd. Besides, she would never have forgotten someone like A.J.

"Okay, well, I moved here two years ago to start teaching history at the high school. Your aunt was my mentor that first year, and she invited me to go to church with her." He shrugged. "I said yes and kept saying yes when they asked me to help with stuff."

"It sounds like you keep pretty busy."

"I do, but that's the way I like it. The thought of sitting around by myself all day." He shuddered at the thought. "I can't do that. I need to be active or I go crazy."

"I bet you were a real joy to have in the classroom as a child." She smirked sarcastically.

A.J. barked a laugh. "Not at all. But I made up for it with my charm." He wiggled his eyebrows, and Madeleine had to giggle.

"Where did you live before here?" She wanted to know everything about this man. Something about him intrigued her immensely.

"Little Rock." He waved his hands. "I mean, college, really. But Little Rock is where I grew up and where my family lives."

"Do you have a big family?"

"No. It's average, I guess. I have two younger sisters, two parents, one dog. We're pretty normal."

"Do you get along with them? Your family?"

"Yeah … I get along with my sisters pretty well." He

chuckled. "Much better than I did when we all lived at home together."

Hmmm. He didn't say anything about his parents.

"Enough about me. What about you? How did you decide to become an artist?"

Madeleine sighed. "I've always loved art, ever since I was a little girl. After we moved to Kansas City, I visited art museums on field trips. I took some classes at school and begged my mom to let me sign up for art camps." She pulled at a strand of hair. "I was over the moon when I got into art school ... until I found out how difficult it was. I worked my tail off the last four years, and I am so glad to be done."

A bird flew overhead and landed in the tree above them. Madeleine gazed at the azure sky and the verdant trees.

"You know, it feels weird to call myself an artist—like I need to have a painting hanging in a museum in order to say that—but my professors really pounded that into me in college. You are an artist." She banged the table for emphasis. "So, I am an artist."

"I wish I had something like that, a goal I'd always worked toward. I really love being a teacher and working with kids, but I don't think I'm going to teach forever. I just haven't figured out what I want to be when I grow up." He laughed at his own joke, for the second time that evening, tasting the chocolate ice cream from his bowl. "This is amazing."

"I know. I'm very impressed at Sam's cooking skills." She'd given herself an extra helping of Sam's browned butter pecan, and the flavor turned out to be her favorite. Potlucks were definitely one of the things she missed about church.

A.J.'s words still rattled around in her brain. "So, you don't have any dreams or goals?"

"I've had plenty over the years, but nothing's stuck yet. Maybe I'll never figure it out. I'll just hop from one job to the next."

That sounded terrible. Without thinking, she said, "Maybe I

can help you figure it out." Wait, what? Her brain sounded an alarm in rebellion. Do not get invested! You're only here for the summer!

A.J. grinned. "All right. You can be my life coach and find a career for me."

Life. Coach. Oh, goodness.

Madeleine turned to dessert for comfort. Her spoon scraped the bottom as she tried to scoop up the very last bits of her ice cream. She made a small frown at the empty bowl.

"How about I throw that away for you?" A.J. stood with his own empty bowl and reached for hers, too.

Madeleine waited for a moment while he took their trash away but watched as he got cornered by an older lady wanting to talk. A.J., who'd been calm and upbeat every time she'd seen him, scowled and squirmed where he stood. She wanted to grab another bottle of water anyway, and she thought she might help him get out of what appeared to be the beginning of a long conversation.

As she approached from behind the woman, Madeleine could hear a little of what she said.

"I normally wouldn't say anything, but I know you don't have your family here to watch out for you. You need to be careful about who you hang around. That young lady is not a Christian and isn't someone you need to be dating. I know you were probably just being friendly, but I want to make sure neither of you gets hurt."

Madeleine resisted the urge to clean out her ears. She wouldn't believe what she was hearing, except that she knew this particular lady. Nancy Jones. The same woman who'd hurt her mother so much all those years ago. Madeleine's heart beat faster, and her blood pressure rose as she searched for a place to hide. She took deep breaths, trying not to cry. I should not be this emotional! I barely even know A.J. But

Madeleine knew there was more to her reaction than her

crush on A.J. This was turning into exactly what her mother had warned her about. Finally, Madeleine found her aunt chatting with a cluster of ladies and mustered up enough courage to talk without crying.

"I'm gonna walk home, I think." Madeleine plastered a pleasant expression on her face.

"Is everything okay?" Clara asked, her brow wrinkled in concern. "Yeah, it's a nice night, and I've had my fill of ice cream. I'd like to take a walk and get to bed early." Madeleine did her best to use a happy, casual voice. She threw in her biggest disarming smile to seal the deal.

"Okay. I'll just be a little longer. Sure you don't need a ride?"

"No, I'll see you at the house. Bye!" Madeleine walked away before Clara could dig too much deeper.

7

O ne minute, A.J. had left Madeleine at their picnic table, and the next, she was gone. A.J. scanned the crowd, thinking maybe

she'd gone to talk to someone else. He circulated the pavilion, hoping to catch a glimpse of her. "Weird."

Spotting Clara, A.J. walked over to her. "Hey, have you seen Madeleine? I was talking to her, and then ..." He waved his hand like a magician performing a disappearing trick.

Clara pursed her lips. "I'm sorry, she just left. I think she wasn't feeling well."

Weird. She hadn't seemed at all unwell a few minutes ago.

A.J. tried to erase any disappointment from his face. Clara would pounce on whatever slight spark of interest he might show in her niece. "Thanks, Clara. I guess I'll catch her another time." He gave a little wave and walked away.

He thought back to what Nancy had told him. At the time, he'd brushed off her warning as nothing to be concerned about. He knew better than to get tangled romantically with someone who wasn't a Christian, especially when he barely knew her. But Madeleine's sudden disappearance had him thinking.

He was worried about her. And to be honest, he was more than a little offended she hadn't thought to say goodbye before leaving. A.J. briefly considered running after Madeleine. If she'd only just left, he could easily catch up with her. Even though he wasn't currently training with students, A.J. kept in shape year-round and was certain he could outpace her.

But if Madeleine had any more to say to him, she would've stuck around. Something caused Madeleine to leave in a hurry. A.J. only wished he could figure out what that was.

The evening was cool, and the walk was not terribly long, so Madeleine didn't get too hot. About halfway through, she slipped off her espadrilles and strolled barefoot through the grass. She actually enjoyed the time alone, just her and the crickets, a few fireflies blinking on as she got closer to the house. After the walk and a warm bath, Madeleine was much calmer. Enough that she knew she'd been silly for getting so upset in the first place.

As Madeleine pulled on her pajamas, the kitchen door opened downstairs. Time to face Aunt Clara. She racked her brain for an excuse for her sudden disappearance as she walked down the stairs, but nothing would come.

"I wasn't completely honest with you. There was something that made me upset." Madeleine helped her aunt unpack the empty tubs of ice cream.

"I thought so. What happened?" Aunt Clara squeezed Madeleine's hand before turning to fill the sink.

"It was Nancy Jones ... of course." Madeleine rolled her eyes.

"Tell me." Aunt Clara's reply was brief, but she scrubbed the dishes with excessive vigor.

"I overheard her warning A.J. to stay away from me."

Madeleine grabbed a towel and took a tub from her aunt. "I don't know what I ever did to make that lady hate me so much."

"I'm sorry, sweetie. That must have been very hurtful." Clara gave

Madeleine a warm hug, squeezing her shoulders as she pulled away. Without asking, she began to fill the kettle and pulled chamomile tea from the pantry. Aunt Clara always had a box of chamomile ready for situations like this. There had been many nights spent in conversation over a cup in this very kitchen.

"It was. I think if it had been anyone else, I could've brushed it off, but hearing her talk about me … it just made me so angry." Madeleine hopped up on a barstool at the kitchen island to watch her aunt make the tea.

"What did you say to her?"

Madeleine stared at her aunt in confusion. "Nothing. I don't think either of them know I heard the conversation."

"Hmm." Clara pulled two mugs down from the cabinet and dropped a tea bag in each.

"What?" Madeleine knew from experience that Clara wasn't going to leave this alone. She always had some advice to impart. Whether or not Madeleine chose to take that advice was another matter entirely.

"Well, if it were me, I would confront her."

"Really? Why?" Madeleine could see no reason to endure further humiliation at the hands of Nancy Jones.

"How can she apologize to you if she doesn't know she's hurt you?" Clara reached for the whistling kettle and poured steaming water into both cups. She stirred a smidgen of honey into one and a generous portion into the other, handing the second cup to Madeleine.

Madeleine breathed in the sweet smell of her tea and wrapped her hands around the warm mug as she thought. Did

Nancy deserve the chance to apologize? Would she even ask for forgiveness, given the chance?

"I need to think about it," Madeleine said, finally. That was the best she could do for now.

"That's all I ask. And if you do decide to talk to her, tomorrow morning at church would be a great time."

Madeleine sighed and massaged her temples. She was too tired to argue about whether or not she would attend church services.

"Why is it so important to you that I go to church? If I believe in God, can't I worship in my own way?" This was something Madeleine had always wondered and never asked. Why couldn't Aunt Clara leave her alone? Just because she didn't do things Clara's way didn't mean Madeleine didn't have faith.

"It's important to me—and it's important to God—that you follow God the way He intended. That you get baptized, that you become a Christian, and that you become a part of the church Jesus gave His life for." Clara's eyes shone with an intense sincerity. She'd obviously thought about this before, too. "It's like ..." She gestured out to the garden. "It's like making sure my plants are in good soil. If you surround yourself with God's people, you'll grow. We're all better when we work together."

"I'll come with you in the morning. Because I love you." Madeleine drank the last sip from her cup. "And because I want to keep my job."

Aunt Clara laughed. "I love you, too, Maddy." As Madeleine turned to leave, Clara quickly added, "Oh, you should know, A.J. asked about you." The sparkle in her eye told Madeleine that Aunt Clara was more than a little pleased to share that.

"Oh? I guess I should have said something to him before I left. I'll try to catch him at church tomorrow."

"I'm sure he would like that very much." Clara's grin spread from ear to ear.

Before going to bed, Madeleine cracked open the Bible waiting where she'd left it on the nightstand. She read through a sermon on praying and found that she remembered most of The Lord's Prayer, but she stopped cold when she read the next two verses. "For if you forgive others their trespasses, your heavenly Father will also forgive you, but if you do not forgive others their trespasses, neither will your Father forgive your trespasses."

She had not forgiven Nancy Jones. If there had been any doubt in her mind before, it all came crashing back when she had the smallest run-in with the woman. To be honest, a small part of her held the whole church responsible for abandoning her mother in her time of need.

But if God wouldn't forgive her unless she forgave them … Madeleine sighed. She needed to think about this. A lot.

8

"*A*h, finally." A.J. had just gotten the last door unlocked for morning services. The front lock always gave him a bit of trouble, and this Sunday was no different. He checked that the lights and the air conditioning were flipped on in the auditorium and warmed up the computer in the AV booth.

A.J. usually arrived at the church building before anyone else for worship. He didn't do everything for the small congregation, but he did quite a lot. Not that he minded. A.J. had always enjoyed coming to worship services. He loved greeting friends new and old, singing together, praying together, and learning more about God. His parents even had a stack of video tapes of him preaching sermons and leading singing as a little boy.

This particular morning, A.J. found Sam already at the building. The preacher was sitting at the desk in his office with his head bowed. A.J. treaded as lightly as he could, but Sam sat up and smiled at him as he walked past the door.

"Morning, A.J." Sam beckoned for A.J. to join him. "I'm just getting the sermon ready."

"What's it about?" A.J. sat in one of two chairs facing the

desk. "About twenty minutes." Sam stared at him with a twinkle in his eye.

A.J. groaned instinctively. What a terrible joke.

"I'm preaching on fellowship and togetherness." Sam's face shifted to a more serious expression. "I've been reminded recently of the trouble we can get into when we let division set in. Madeleine Mullins reminded me, actually." Sam paused, drumming his fingers on the table. "I know I can't make the decision for her, and I can't simply will her into conversion. Clara told me she was close to accepting Christ before her parents' divorce. I just wish I could convince her the church isn't out to get her."

A.J. nodded. "She seems nice—and definitely not closed off to Christianity. You know, Nancy Jones told me I need to stay away from her since she's not a Christian yet."

"What do you think?" Sam was never one to let A.J. off easily. If he were a colleague, he'd be a big believer in teachable moments. Come to think of it, Sam was a teacher in a way. He'd certainly educated A.J. a lot in the past two years.

A.J. took a deep breath. "I think she'll never come to church if the church members won't be friends with her. I know it doesn't have to be me, but—for better or worse—we've hit it off."

"Guarding your heart is not unwise, A.J. You can't bank on her changing her mind. And she won't appreciate a friendship that comes with strings attached." Direct advice from Sam was not common, so A.J. knew he shouldn't take it lightly. But he also couldn't give up on a friendship with Madeleine yet.

"I know, I know. I've thought about all this. I still think I want to take the chance. We're just friends, and I would like to keep her friendship."

A.J. hadn't fully made up his mind, but now that he heard the words come out of his mouth, he knew he believed them.

"All right, son. But take things slow, for your own sake. Now you'd better get out of my office and let me finish praying. I need all the help I can get, and you need to get the building ready for services." Sam rose and gently shooed A.J. out of the office.

About half an hour later as church members began trickling in for class, A.J. caught himself looking for Madeleine to appear. He eventually had to stop searching to head over to the teen room and get his own class started. By the time A.J. pulled the kids away from conversation and herded them into the auditorium after class, he'd convinced himself Madeleine would not be there that morning. That's what he'd expected anyway. But his heart leapt when he saw a young woman with wavy, golden-brown hair standing beside Clara. A smile grew across his face.

"What are you so happy about all of a sudden?" Mitchell asked from beside him.

"Nothing. I mean—just happy to be with you, Mitchell. Can't I be happy to be with my main man Mitchell?" Obviously, he wasn't fooling anyone, because Mitchell was already staring toward Madeleine with a glint in his eyes.

"I think someone has a crush!" Mitchell punched him in the arm. A few more kids gaped at them. Teenagers weren't usually good with subtlety.

"Shush, shh." Truth be told, A.J. wasn't that discreet himself. "We're just friends. I barely know her. We've only ever talked, like, twice." He was slipping into teen jargon. That was never good. "Be cool, man. Okay? Be mature."

"Cool. I'll be cool. No problem." The mischievous expression on Mitchell's face made A.J. nervous, but there wasn't a lot he could do about that. He'd already made eye contact with Madeleine and couldn't back away now.

"Hey, A.J." Madeleine shot him a smile. He fought to catch his breath. "Good morning, Madeleine."

Mitchell tugged on A.J.'s arm before he could say anything more. Mr.

Simpson was standing at the pulpit, ready to give the announcements. "Guess I'll see you after." He nodded to Madeleine before following

Mitchell to the auditorium.

A.J. mentally chided himself for getting so excited to see Madeleine. He'd told Sam he would take things slow with her, and he intended to keep that promise. Nancy was right to warn him. The effect Madeleine was having on him must be obvious to everyone. The last thing he wanted was to develop feelings for someone who didn't love Jesus as much as he did. That could only end in disaster.

Through the singing and Sam's sermon on fellowship and the body of Christ, A.J. made a concerted effort to focus his mind and his spirit. He needed an extra dose of wisdom this morning. The kind that could only come from listening to the word of God and surrounding himself with fellow Christians.

Sam's sermon focused on several Bible verses about togetherness. He started with Matthew 18:20, "For where two or three are gathered in my name, there I am among them." Too often, A.J. had heard this verse used to claim that a couple of Christians constituted a church service. But Sam argued that context showed it meant powerful things could happen when Christian brothers and sisters work together for God's glory. A.J. let Sam's message and the words of God wash over him and return him to center.

After services, A.J. waited and let others greet Madeleine first. He visited with the teens, reminding them about their float trip on Monday morning. When he spotted Madeleine looking around as if for a way out, A.J. saw his opening and stepped in.

"So, what did you think? First church service in a while, huh?"

"Yeah. Thankfully, none of the songs in the songbook have changed, although the projector is new." Madeleine nodded to the screen at the front of the auditorium.

She must have been gone a long time. There weren't many churches left that didn't use a projector.

"Hey, I wanted to remind you about the float trip in the morning.

You still in?"

"Yeah …" A shadow of worry crossed her face.

"You aren't going to back out on me, are you?" A.J.'s voice betrayed his disappointment.

"It's just … I haven't been canoeing in a really long time." Madeleine bit her lip. He'd never noticed her lips before.

"Don't worry about it. You can ride with me." The words came out before he really thought it through, but Madeleine looked pleased with the idea.

"You sure I won't slow you down?"

"Of course not. Besides, it's not a race. We're just going to have fun."

"Okay. But don't say I didn't warn you." An enticing glint flashed in her eyes.

"Consider me warned." He probably had a big, dopey grin plastered across his face. "I'll text you the details this afternoon."

"Great. Thanks!"

Man, that girl had a pretty smile. He had better watch out.

* * *

After lunch on Sunday, Madeleine set to work drawing her vision for the mural. Aunt Clara and the other church members were meeting in small groups for the evening, so she would be able to work the rest of the day without interruption. She'd arranged to meet with Sam in the morning before the float trip, and canoeing down the river with A.J. wouldn't take too much time away from her work. Was she imagining things, or was A.J. almost as eager as she was to spend more time together? As far as Madeleine could tell, A.J. was not aware she'd overheard his conversation with Nancy the night before. And she was fine keeping it that way. No need to create unnecessary conflict. Aunt Clara would say she wasn't being open and honest, but Madeleine chose to squash that little voice in her head and move forward.

Fresh out of ideas, Madeleine set down her pad and pencil to read a little more of Matthew. Jesus had just finished preaching a sermon and was coming down the mountain. Madeleine read story after story of Jesus healing all kinds of people. Women and men, a family member of His friend, a Roman soldier's servant, a man with leprosy, a girl who was dead.

Woven in with these stories were teachings of Jesus that were hard to understand. People must give up everything to follow God. Being a good Jew is no guarantee of getting into heaven. Jesus came for the sinners, not the righteous.

She read about how Jesus called Matthew. If she hadn't had that conversation with Sam at the sandwich shop, she would've completely missed the significance of Matthew being a tax collector. That must have been a big shock to everyone else when Jesus started hanging out with tax collectors and fishermen. Not exactly Ivy League material.

Madeleine was struck again and again by how quickly Jesus handed out forgiveness and healing to the people around Him. Poor or rich. A close friend or a stranger. Jesus touched them all.

The idea of Jesus touching all people took root in her mind. Madeleine mulled it over as she went downstairs to make a cup of peppermint tea. When she returned to her desk, she was ready to trash her other sketches and draw out a new plan. She divided the page into quadrants and labeled each with a different miracle or event she'd read about in Matthew.

Madeleine spent the rest of the evening laboring over small sketches of each vignette she wanted to paint on the wall. She eventually compiled everything into a large to-scale draft she could bring to Sam in the morning. The clock read midnight by the time Madeleine finally got to bed that night, but pride and assurance buoyed her spirits. Sam was going to love what she had to show him.

As Madeleine washed and got dressed for bed, she glanced at her phone. A text message from A.J. had come in a couple hours ago that she'd completely missed.

A.J.: Hey, Madeleine. Great to see you at church this morning. We're meeting at the building at 8. Wear clothes and shoes you don't mind getting wet. Bring a bottle of water and $30.

Wow. Madeleine very much regretted agreeing to go on this trip. Thirty dollars was kind of a lot. She'd already planned to get up at seven to meet with Sam. She would have to worry about finding shoes and a water bottle in the morning. She sure hoped some quality time with a cute guy would make up for all this trouble.

9

In the morning, Madeleine pulled out a T-shirt and shorts she usually wore for working out. She put those on over her swimsuit and found a cheap pair of flip-flops. As she rummaged around the kitchen for a water bottle, Clara padded down the stairs.

"Searching for something?" She rubbed the sleep from her puffy eyes.

"Sorry, Aunt Clara! I didn't mean to be so loud. Um, do you have any water bottles?"

"Here." Clara pulled open a cabinet by the sink that was full of lunch boxes and travel mugs and plastic tumblers. Madeleine chose the most durable-looking bottle to fill with ice and water.

"Getting ready for your canoeing trip?" Aunt Clara ran her fingers through her short hair, taming it a little.

"Yes! How do I look? Outdoorsy?" Madeleine posed, hands on her hips.

"Do you need water shoes?"

"What?" Madeleine glanced down to her foam flip-flops. "No, I'm sure these will work fine."

"I think I have a pair in the closet." Aunt Clara turned to go upstairs to her bedroom before Madeleine could stop her. She returned with the most hideous shoes Madeleine had ever seen. They probably used to be green—maybe blue—but now they were a washed-out yellowish color that resembled snot. The soles seemed sturdy, but the fabric on the sides was frayed and worn. There was no way in the world Madeleine was wearing those shoes in a canoe with A.J.

"Wow. Those are … well-loved." Madeleine racked her brain for ideas to get her out of this situation.

"Try them on. What size do you wear?" Aunt Clara thrust the offensive footwear into Madeleine's hands.

"Six. These are probably too big." Please be too big. Please be too big.

"I think they're a size seven, but they might run small. Try them on." She waved her hands in impatience.

Hesitant, Madeleine kicked off her flip-flops and gingerly slipped on the water shoes, hoping there wasn't any dormant toe fungus hiding out inside of them.

"Ta-da! A perfect fit." Clara grinned triumphantly.

"All right. Well, maybe I'll put them on once we get our canoes." Or maybe she'd hide them in the car and toss them in a trash can somewhere. Or burn them in a bonfire.

"Okay. Do you need anything else? Sunscreen? Sunglasses? I have some on a string so they won't fall into the water. Polarized. They used to belong to your Uncle George."

"Thank you so much for your help, but I really need to hurry. I have a meeting with Sam this morning to show him my first draft of the mural."

"Really? Can I see?" Clara's whole face lit up with excitement.

Madeleine just couldn't refuse her. She rolled the paper out onto the kitchen island and waited for a reaction.

"Oh, Maddy! It's wonderful!"

Madeleine's chest swelled a little as she watched Clara pore over the drawing. If Aunt Clara liked it, then maybe Sam would, too. The better to finish this job quickly, of course.

By the time Madeleine finally got out of the house and over to the church building, she was five minutes late for her meeting with Sam.

Not very professional, but she got the impression that Sam was an understanding man. And she was hopeful her mural rendering would be good enough to win his goodwill.

"Hmm," Sam said when she rolled out the drawing on his office desk. Not quite the reaction she'd been expecting. "It's a very good start, Madeleine."

A good start? Madeleine had been hoping to begin sketching outlines on the wall tomorrow. How long would this project take?

"What is it you don't like?" Best to get straight to the point and figure out what the client wanted.

"I like all that you have here. I just think it's missing something. You have the miracles of Jesus and the people Jesus touched. But I need to see His sacrifice and sovereignty," he said. "It's not enough to show Jesus was a good man. We need to see that Jesus is God." Sam searched her eyes, but he obviously didn't find what he wanted there.

Madeleine was reminded of being back in school and disappointing her professors. She had no idea what he meant, no idea what Sam wanted her to say.

"Would you like a cross? Jesus on the cross?" Christians liked crosses.

She knew that much.

"That would be a start. The cross is critical. Right in the middle here, perhaps." Sam paused. "Have you been reading Matthew?"

"I finished chapter nine last night. I'm taking it slow, I guess." Madeleine examined the books on the shelf, avoiding eye contact and wishing she could tell Sam she'd read more.

"That's good. If you read too fast, you'll miss so much. But you should keep reading. I can see how your interpretation of the scriptures is reflected in your drawings." Sam studied the paper again, reaching out to touch faces and trees and water Madeleine had painstakingly sketched the night before.

She rubbed her temples. There was a fine line between pleasing a client and becoming too emotionally attached to her work. She usually had more creative freedom than this job was allowing. But if reading the rest of Matthew would make Sam happy, she would do it.

"If I want to get started drawing this on the wall soon, I'll have to pick up the pace with my reading. But I can at least get the wall washed tonight and primed tomorrow."

"Do you need any money? For primer and paint?" Sam searched the drawers of his desk, mumbling a little to himself.

"I usually include the cost of materials in my bill, but since this is a different sort of project, I wouldn't mind some funds upfront."

"Ah! Here it is!" Sam pulled an envelope from between two books on top of his desk. Tapping the contents into his hand, Madeleine saw a credit card. "You can borrow the church card. Just make sure to keep all your receipts."

"Thank you." Madeleine slipped the card into her wallet, likely a much safer location than its previous home in Sam's office.

A door creaked open somewhere in the building. Madeleine startled a bit, even after her embarrassing encounter with A.J. last week. The dark and empty rooms creeped her out.

"Hello! I am not an intruder! Please do not injure me!" A.J. called out into the echoing hallway.

Madeleine shrugged at Sam's questioning expression and poked her head out of the office.

"Thank you for not sneaking up on me again."

"Ready to explore new lands in our canoe, Sacajawea?" A.J.

grabbed either side of the door frame, bouncing on the balls of his feet, eyebrows raised in excitement.

"Does that make you Lewis or Clark?" Two could play the historical trivia game.

"Clark, obviously." A.J. pointed to his red hair. "Besides, I would never voluntarily take the name Merriweather."

"Mary is a lovely name." Madeleine giggled. "I happen to have a grandmother named Mary."

"Don't you two have somewhere to be?" The smirk on Sam's face did not match his irritated tone.

"Yes, sir. I filled the bus with gas, and I'm expecting the rest of the group in a few minutes. Now I'm getting everything loaded and ready to go. Wanna come help me?" A.J. turned to Madeleine.

"Sure … that is, if you don't have anything else to add?" Madeleine shot a glance to Sam.

"No. Let's meet again on Wednesday to talk some more." Sam shooed her away with a flick of his hands.

"Sounds fine. See you then." Madeleine took off down the hall after A.J.

Their first stop was in the kitchen to pack ice and lunch supplies. A.J. gave directions to Madeleine as they pulled peanut butter, jelly, and bread from grocery sacks on the counter, then assembled a small stack of sandwiches. Madeleine couldn't help but think they made a pretty good team. In a short time, they had everything loaded into two small coolers and packed in the church bus.

While they'd been working, several teens had arrived in the parking lot and more trickled in as they waited. Apparently, Madeleine had been wrong about how much time she'd be spending with the youth group. Learning everyone's names might actually be helpful. She remembered Mitchell, Sophie, and Caitlin from the ice cream social. And Jessica she recognized from the sandwich shop. Turner, Emma, Ethan, Dylan, Joshua, and Phoebe she met for the first time.

They all made an effort to welcome her, asking her questions. She tried to reciprocate by learning a little about them, but the information overload was overwhelming. Madeleine ended up just smiling and nodding until it was time to get on the bus.

The drive to the Buffalo River would take about an hour. A.J. focused on driving, and the teenagers were friendly but spoke in their own language of inside jokes and pop culture references Madeleine couldn't follow. Still smarting from her conversation with Sam, Madeleine decided to read a little more of Matthew. She hadn't brought Sam's massive Bible, but she quickly found an app on her phone that would do the trick.

She picked up again with people questioning Jesus. The Pharisees and other Jewish leaders were opposing Him at every turn. Jesus taught about heaven and what it was like to follow God. He compared it to treasure and pearls and like being picked out of a net of fish. Over and over again she read about the righteous people living with God and the unrighteous living in a place with "weeping and gnashing of teeth." Was she unrighteous? Would she be weeping and gnashing her teeth?

Finally, Madeleine came to the transfiguration of Jesus, when He was transformed into something else, shining bright and white like the sun, and the voice of God spoke from a cloud. Could she really believe all of this? That the Son of God came down to Earth as a human? That He performed miracles? That God spoke through clouds?

And if she did, was she really following God the way she should? Didn't a God like that deserve her undivided attention and not a vague promise to follow Him sometime in the future?

Madeleine was jolted into the present as A.J. turned off the paved highway and onto a dirt road that felt like it was made entirely of ridges and potholes. Madeleine shook the thoughts clouding her head and stretched her arms and neck.

"Here we are! Wait here and I'll go pay inside." A.J. bounded off with their money and release forms.

A young man from the canoe rental company came outside to get everyone's equipment ready. Six canoes, each a different hue, were stacked in a trailer behind a pickup truck. They followed the truck onto the highway and down more country roads until they reached a dock.

"Let's go, people!" A.J. was way too excited, but his enthusiasm was catching.

Madeleine smiled at the teens, all laughter and talking. Did they ever stop talking? She followed them off the bus single file.

The canoe man handed each of them a life jacket, which they were required to wear. Madeleine's smelled like it had been well-used by lots of very sweaty people. After everyone had donned their jackets, they gathered to listen to instructions on proper steering, how to right a flipped canoe, and basically how to not die while on the water. Madeleine frowned in what she hoped was an intelligent manner, but her brain spun at the sheer volume of information being thrown at it.

She sincerely hoped she didn't have to use any of the lifesaving tips the young man was giving.

Finally, they broke off into pairs. Madeleine and A.J. watched each group push off into the river and waited until they were the only ones left. They waded out with their canoe. Madeleine climbed in while A.J. held the boat steady and pushed it out into the water. He deftly climbed in, and they pushed their oars against the rocky ground until they were floating in open water.

Madeleine tried her best to follow A.J.'s lead although she was sitting in the front. She cut her oars into the water as smoothly as she could manage, remembering the crash course in canoeing they'd received minutes ago. For a long while, her oar did nothing but slap the water and splash uselessly. The boat slowly inched forward in fits and starts. Madeleine huffed impatiently, but tried again and again, each time making slight progress. She watched A.J.'s oar soundlessly slice the water and mimicked his motions as best she could. After a few minutes, they fell into a comfortable rhythm, and the canoe glided along the river with a bit more grace.

Once they caught up with the teens, Madeleine was able to relax a little and enjoy the beautiful day. On either side of the river were cliffs and big, magnificent trees. Some on shore, some sprouting out of the cliff face at right angles. Every once in a while, houses appeared with weathered docks and small rowboats. The weather was warm, but an occasional cool breeze floated over the water, and the partially cloudy sky kept the heat from becoming unbearable.

A ray of white light broke through the clouds overhead and shone through the trees and onto the river. The water glittered as the sunlight was reflected a million times. Madeleine couldn't fully look without squinting.

She thought over the Bible passage she'd just read. What must the apostles have been feeling when they saw Jesus appearing like a bright beam of sunlight? Peter had confessed that Jesus was the Son of God. But what God was this? How powerful was God, really? And who was Jesus? Madeleine was even more muddled than before she'd started to read Matthew. Each dive into the Bible left her with more questions than answers.

With nothing else to distract her, Madeleine dwelled on her thoughts of Jesus and the Bible. The miracles and the radical teachings, not to mention the voice of God coming down from heaven, all had Madeleine thinking she'd never taken the Bible seriously enough. There had been a point in her life when she'd considered getting baptized. She'd grown up going to church and watched her older friends make the decision to dedicate themselves to God, but then … then her dad left, and piece by piece, her whole world fell apart. After that, Madeleine had pushed God aside to deal with the bigger problems of her life. But maybe that had been the wrong choice. Maybe God was actually the biggest thing. Ever. Maybe she had everything completely backward and upside down.

Madeleine slowly came out of the shell of her mind and realized she'd been rowing with A.J. the whole time, not saying a word, completely lost in her thoughts. She turned to him and gave a small smile. Partly to apologize for being so quiet, partly to check he wasn't ready to jump out of the canoe in boredom. He returned her smile but didn't say anything. Amazingly, A.J. was totally fine to sit quietly with her. He hadn't struck her as the silent type, but maybe he was comfortable enough with her that he didn't need to talk. That thought made Madeleine smile even more.

"How's it going back there?" she called to him.

"Great. You're not as bad at this as you made me think," A.J. replied. "Those instructions we got must have really worked. I think I'm an expert now. Maybe I should join a rowing team." Madeleine turned to A.J., rocking the boat slightly. She did her best to balance out her weight and still the canoe.

"Whoa there. I said you're not bad. I didn't say you're good," A.J. teased.

Madeleine laughed. With all the heavy thoughts weighing on her mind, having a casual conversation with someone—a very handsome someone, no less—was nice.

"Thanks for tagging along with me." A.J.'s voice rang out over the river.

"I'm glad I did. And I'm glad I got the coveted seat in the youth minister's canoe." This time she called over her shoulder without attempting to turn around.

A.J. barked a laugh. "Quite the opposite. There's no way I could convince one of them to sit with me. You definitely got the worst seat in the house."

"Oh, I don't think so. Not at all."

10

*T*hey had been on the water about an hour when they came to a wider section of the river. On the shore, there was a dock

and stairs leading to a rope swing hanging off an old, gnarled tree. The teens circled their canoes, and some jumped into the river. Their surroundings were almost completely still, aside from the splashing and kicking churning up the water. A few of the boys climbed up to the rope swing and jumped off, shouting in pure joy as they soared through the air and into the cool water below.

A.J. and Madeleine steered their canoe parallel to the shore where they could supervise the teens. Mitchell and Dylan swam over after taking their turn jumping in the river.

"Aren't you going to get in?" Mitchell held onto the edge of their boat. His short, blond hair was spiked from the water, giving him an impish and dangerous air.

"Who's going to dive in and save you when one of you dorks hits your head on a rock?" A.J. splashed the boys, teasing.

"C'mon, A.J.," Dylan pleaded. "The water's great."

"Hey, guys, why don't you go bug someone else?" Madeleine chimed in.

Mitchell and Dylan both hung from the side of their canoe, and the boat started to sway.

"What? You scared?" Mitchell's eyes gleamed in a way that made Madeleine very nervous.

"A little, yes. Please stop." Nothing Madeleine said could deter the two boys. While A.J. laughed and joked with Mitchell and Dylan, Madeleine knew in the pit of her stomach she was not going to like what came next.

"Hey, come here, Turner," Mitchell called over his shoulder before throwing Madeleine a wicked grin.

Turner swam from where he was splashing around with Emma and Sophie to join them. "What's going on?"

Madeleine was sure Turner wouldn't harass them like the others. He seemed like such a sweet guy.

"Tell A.J. he needs to jump in," Dylan said.

"A.J., you need to jump in." Turner nodded in mock seriousness.

The three boys paused. A silent conversation passed between them. Madeleine's heart sank into her stomach. Without saying a word, they simultaneously pushed down on the canoe as hard as they could and let go. In one clean motion, the boat flipped backward into the water.

Madeleine screamed. Water surged in her mouth and nose. Her feet scraped rocks. Her shoes tugged on her toes.

Thanks to the smelly, orange life vest, Madeleine bobbed up to the surface at once. She coughed out the river water and surveyed the damage around her. Their canoe was still upside down. Her hair was wet but stayed pulled into a ponytail. Her feet were bare, but a quick scan of the area revealed two black flip flops floating on the water beside her.

Madeleine plucked her flip flops out of the water and

clumsily shoved them on her feet. But as she waded through the water, her right shoe fell off again.

"What in the world?" Madeleine lifted the shoe up to her face. Her flip flop was broken. The shoe had been cheap. Only one dollar if she remembered correctly. But still, it was the only shoe she had right now.

Except ... no, Madeleine had left Aunt Clara's water shoes in her car. Yep. Now she was down to one shoe for the rest of the trip. Great.

A strange sound echoed off the water. Was that A.J.? Was he ... laughing? A.J. and the boys all swam in a small cluster, slapping each other on the back. And they were not chuckling nervously but giving great big guffaws.

White hot anger simmered inside Madeleine's chest. Well, fine. If he enjoyed that so much, he could be the one to flip the canoe right side up. "Hey! If you're done goofing off, I could use some help getting in my canoe." Madeleine's voice contained more than a hint of irritability. The boys looked over, a little sheepish but mostly giddy.

"You shouldn't have been so rough, you know. My shoe is broken because of you." Maybe she was milking this a little, but she hadn't gotten anything even close to an apology yet.

"Sorry, Madeleine." Turner's face fell into a penitent frown.

"Yeah, that stinks." Dylan gave a half-hearted pout of his lip. Although his apology wasn't as genuine as Madeleine would've liked, she was still willing to forgive.

"C'mon, that was not our fault. It was an accident." Mitchell probably would have stomped his feet had he not been treading water.

"An accident that wouldn't have happened if you had listened and left us alone." Madeleine was not willing to let this go. She was wet and miserable and grew angrier the more she thought about it.

"You need to loosen up a bit and have some fun." Mitchell's

jaw jutted out. He kicked his legs, putting some distance between them.

A.J. waded over, a stupid smile on his face. Her simmering anger grew to a boil at seeing how much he was enjoying this.

"You guys go bother someone else." He waved the boys away. "Hey, are you okay?" A.J.'s voice showed a little sympathy, even if he didn't share in her anger.

"Yeah, I'm sorry." Madeleine was still indignant but tried to appear rational. She blew out a breath, and her blood pressure lessened a little. She smoothed out her wrinkled brow. "I know none of this is your fault."

"No, but it's not that big of a deal. It's amazing we haven't had more canoes flip today. The water actually feels kind of nice."

"What? I can't believe you don't care they tipped us. That was so immature!" Her face grew hot. "It's the principle of the thing, A.J. If Mitchell will just apologize, then I'll be happy to let it go."

"And what if he doesn't apologize?"

"Well, aren't you going to make him?" The thought hadn't occurred to her that A.J. might not intervene.

"I'm going to talk to him. They all need to learn about boundaries and respect, but I can't make him apologize. That's something he has to decide to do on his own." A.J. swam away before Madeleine could say any more.

Madeleine limped in her one good shoe onto the rocky shore and sat to watch the boys attempt to right the canoe. If she wasn't still angry, she would probably find the scene pretty humorous. Joshua and Ethan got in their boat and pulled the edge of hers in between them. The canoe must be heavy from the grunts of the three other teens and A.J. as they awkwardly hoisted it up and flipped it over. The whole process took a while and, when it was all over, Madeleine found she'd cooled off quite a bit.

At this point, Madeleine knew she'd dug herself a hole she couldn't get out of. She had probably overreacted. No, she had definitely overreacted. And now she was embarrassed about the whole thing and desperate to get it behind her so she could enjoy the rest of the day. But she still believed Mitchell owed her some sort of apology before she could forgive him. After all, she had a broken sandal to deal with for the rest of the day.

Sophie and Caitlin joined her on the shore, saving her from having to talk to Mitchell or A.J.

"Hey, there!" Caitlin plopped down on the rocks next to Madeleine, stretching out her legs and tilting her head to fully enjoy the warmth of the sun.

Sophie followed, quiet and graceful, resting on the other side of Madeleine. She reminded Madeleine of a cat she once had. Shadow—the cat—always knew exactly when she needed company and would offer her silent presence as a means of comfort.

The girls were night and day in appearance— Sophie dark and petite, Caitlin tall and fair— and opposites in personality, but somehow the friendship worked.

"Hey, girls. You having a good time?" Madeleine hoped if she asked them about themselves, they wouldn't bring up the canoe-tipping incident.

"Oh, yeah!" Caitlin reminded Madeleine more of a bird. A very loud, chipper bird. "I'm glad A.J. talked us all into this, although I'm surprised he got so many people to come!"

"You always say that," Sophie said from the other side.

"Well, I always am. We're such a flaky group usually." Caitlin laughed. "A.J. is the only reason anyone comes to these activities. We always complain about it." She looked around furtively. "But we secretly love it." Both girls giggled, and Madeleine couldn't help but join in.

"So, what kinds of activities do you usually do together?" What would it be like to be a teenager growing up in a church with other Christians? What would it be like to have a place to belong?

"Oh, all kinds of stuff. We go to the drive-in movies or the roller rink or the mini golf course. Usually something really silly we pretend to hate but actually love," Caitlin answered.

"My favorite thing is the singings," Sophie said.

"Me, too." Caitlin turned to Madeleine conspiratorially. "A.J. has a really nice voice. You should hear him sing sometime."

Madeleine caught herself smiling. The thought of A.J. singing warmed her heart a little.

The girls continued to chat over Madeleine's head. Caitlin's voice loud and bright, Sophie's soft and mellow. Madeleine found her mood much improved by the time the teens decided to continue down the river, despite the fact that she had to walk on the sharp, rocky shore in her bare feet.

"You should've worn some water shoes," A.J. said. "Those things are great for canoeing."

Madeleine rolled her eyes at the perfectly useless suggestion. "You're right, I should have." Her voice held more than a hint of sarcasm, but A.J. was oblivious.

He pulled the right-side-up canoe out to where Madeleine stood in the shallow water and held it steady while she climbed in with as much grace as she could muster. Then she watched with admiration while A.J. yet again hoisted himself athletically into the canoe.

"Doing all right?" A.J. asked, meaning, of course, Have you moved on and forgiven Mitchell? The answer was not quite, but instead she nodded.

"Yep. Sorry I overreacted earlier." Madeleine couldn't bring herself to meet his eyes. He probably thought she was just a silly girl. Too immature to handle a simple outing with teenagers.

"No problem. I hope you're still having fun. I know the boys can be a little rough sometimes." A.J.'s voice softened and sounded unsure. "I had a talk with them, privately."

"Thanks for that." Madeleine turned and smiled at him. "I am having fun. Caitlin and Sophie were telling me all about the crazy trips you take them on. And your great singing voice." She added the last part with a sly grin.

"Oh, really?" He laughed lightly, the tenuous mood broken. "Yeah, they said I need to hear you sing."

"Well, then you should come to our Wednesday night singings."

"I'd like that." Madeleine glanced over her shoulder and found A.J. grinning at her. "You ever think about being a canoe instructor?"

"I can't say that I have. Are you sure that's a job?"

"No, but you'd be great at it."

Around noon, the group made their way to the site of the canoe rental and dragged themselves and their boats out of the water, dripping and giddy with sunshine and exhaustion. Madeleine's feet still hurt, but she tried to put on a brave face.

With the help of Turner, A.J. and Madeleine pulled out the coolers from the bus and passed out sandwiches, water, chips, and some delicious, unhealthy snack cakes. The group naturally divided into boys and girls as they headed over to picnic tables beside the water.

Madeleine enjoyed the chance to spend more time with the girls. The vague, hazy impression she'd formed of the teens at the ice cream social and the bus ride solidified and clarified as she listened to them and observed their personalities. Emma was shy but shared that she and Turner had been dating for over a year. Phoebe was really into theater, and Sophie and Caitlin were in choir. A twinge of guilt stirred in her heart as Madeleine remembered her earlier choice to not bother learning names. She would've missed out on getting to know these incredible kids if she'd remained closed off.

"Have you always lived in Kansas City?" Sophie asked during a lull in the conversation.

"No, I actually lived in Shady Springs when I was younger."

"I thought I remembered you." Sophie smiled. "You and your mom used to help out with Vacation Bible School. My mom is in charge of VBS every summer. If you're still here, I'm sure she'd like to have your help again."

"Sophie Webber?" Madeleine could see her now as a little five-year- old running around the church building, always too shy to talk to adults but willing to let Madeleine give her hugs occasionally. "I didn't recognize you! You're so much ... taller."

All the girls laughed at that. Sophie was just barely five feet, easily the shortest of the group. But Sophie didn't act embarrassed.

"A little," Sophie said. "I hope I'm still not quite finished growing."

"I've been here a while, too," Jessica said from across the table. "But everyone else in the youth group just started coming in the last five years or so. Sam's preaching brought in some new families, and those families brought in more people. And A.J. pulled in a couple more kids from school. Like Dylan and Mitchell."

"The church is a lot bigger than it used to be." Madeleine scanned the riverbank, taking in all of the teens there. "I would've loved to have lots of kids my age at church."

"It's been a blessing." Jessica smiled at the other girls at the table. "I don't know what I'd do without you guys." Her eyes glistened.

Phoebe answered by throwing a chip at her face.

"Hey!" Jessica was knocked out of her sentimental moment and leapt into action, throwing some chips back at Phoebe. By now, all the girls were laughing and tossing chips.

"Whoa, girls!" Madeleine shouted. She should intervene before things got too out of hand.

A piercing whistle rang out over the clearing. "All right, kiddos. Let's clean up and head out." A.J. stood and strode over with a commanding expression on his face. Madeleine knew now what it must be like to be one of the students in his class, getting a lecture for bad behavior. He leaned over with his hands flat on the table and gave each of the girls an intense stare. "And I expect every crumb to be picked up and thrown away."

Somehow, Caitlin still had a handful of chips. She threw the contents of her hand in A.J.'s face and dissolved into a fit of giggles. The entire table froze to watch A.J.'s reaction. Madeleine couldn't help herself. The chip crumbs had landed all over A.J.'s face, on his cheeks, his chin, in his eyebrows. The whole scene was just too hilarious. She collapsed in a heap of laughter, and through her teary eyes, she could see A.J.'s tongue flick out to taste a bit of chip on his lower lip.

His green eyes were bright as he told the girls, "Come on, pick up your trash. We don't have all day."

Madeleine's heart pricked as she wondered how this afternoon would have gone differently if she'd brushed off the canoe tipping with the same good-natured grace that A.J. had. In the scheme of things, an afternoon spent shoeless was not the worst thing in the world. Madeleine would certainly live, and throwing a fit about it didn't change anything. Except perhaps the relationships she was building with these kids.

Once on the bus, the mood was subdued, the teens worn out from the combination of bright sun and water and full bellies. Many of them nodded off, heads resting on windows or shoulders. Up front, A.J. quietly hummed along to the radio. Madeleine stared out her window, watching the trees go by in a blur of green. Eventually, her eyes grew tired, and she pulled up the Bible app on her phone.

Madeleine read about the disciples arguing and Jesus warning them against sin and pride. The combination of harsh words—it's better to cut off your hand or your foot than to sin—and the loving words—you should be like a child, God rejoices over us when we come back—were hard for her to reconcile. But the next section made Madeleine pause.

The heading read, "The Parable of the Unforgiving Servant." Jesus told a story of a man who owed a large amount of money to his king. When he begged for forgiveness, the king erased all his debt. But as soon as that man left, he found another man who owed him a small amount of money and had him thrown into jail, even after he begged for mercy. When the king found out, he was furious and threw the first man into prison. Madeleine's breath caught as she read the last verse. "So also my heavenly Father will do to every one of you, if you do not forgive your brother from your heart."

What counts as a small debt to God? Doesn't everything I go through pale in comparison? Madeleine knew what she had to do next. Please, God, help me do this. Help me to swallow my pride and forgive.

Madeleine checked that A.J. was focused on the road and quickly snuck to the back where Mitchell sat next to a sleeping Dylan. Madeleine waved her hand at him, and Mitchell took the headphones out of his ears.

"Yeah?" His speech was not eloquent, but Mitchell looked at her kindly enough.

"I wanted to say I'm sorry," Madeleine said. "For what?"

"For overreacting earlier. About you tipping our canoe. I shouldn't have gotten so angry. It's not a big deal."

"Yeah … uh, thanks."

Madeleine nodded and, unsure of what to do next, returned to her seat. A.J. glanced at her as she sat.

"Passengers must remain seated at all times, young lady." He gave her a stern stare through the rearview mirror, then softened. "But thanks for doing that. Mitchell isn't a bad guy, really. I'm glad you're on friendly terms again." He turned down the radio a couple notches.

"I didn't know you could hear us."

"Oh, I couldn't. I figured I got the gist of your conversation from watching in the mirror. Was I right? Did you go over to make nice?"

"You were right. I didn't get much out of him, but at least I won't have that weighing on me anymore."

"True." A.J. paused a while and then said, "I heard a quote once. 'Holding a grudge is like drinking poison and then waiting for it to kill your enemy.'"

"Hmm," Madeleine said. What about when you can't forgive? What about when the hurt is like clothing I put on every day? And I'd just as soon walk out of the house without pants on as I'd forgive Mrs. Jones ... or my father? Of course, she couldn't say any of that.

"Hey, thanks for inviting me on the trip. I had a lot of fun." She hoped the change in conversation wouldn't tip A.J. off to her internal struggles.

"I'm glad you came." He gave another of the infectious grins Madeleine had grown to expect. Was this guy always so sunny?

"Me, too." She couldn't help but return the smile.

The time passed quickly as Madeleine and A.J. chatted about the music he was listening to, weather in Arkansas, and the teens. Madeleine could tell from the way he talked that A.J. cared about the kids in the youth group very much. Her heart swelled a little as she realized she was beginning to care about them very much, too ... and maybe a little bit for the part-time youth minister.

11

By the time the white church bus pulled into the parking lot and all the teens were sent home, it was late afternoon.

Madeleine had hoped to put in a lot of work that day, but she realized she might only be able to do a little. Her clothes were dry enough to go out in public without too much embarrassment. And, as much as she hated to admit it, Madeleine was actually glad to have that hideous pair of water shoes in her car. With the card Sam had given her, she hoped to make a trip into town to buy primer and latex paint and other materials from the hardware store.

"What do you have planned for the rest of the day?" A.J. stepped off the bus behind her, carrying a small trash bag.

"I thought I might run to Fayetteville for a shopping trip. Sam gave me the church card." Madeleine smiled mischievously. Impulsively, she added, "Would you like to come along?"

"Um, yeah. Sure." A.J. surveyed the work left to be done. "Let me just finish packing up." He set down the trash bag and unloaded the coolers from the bus.

Madeleine threw her bag into her car and pulled out Aunt Clara's water shoes. They were just as ugly as before, and a day spent in a hot vehicle certainly hadn't improved their smell, but they were still better than nothing. Scrunching her face, Madeleine slipped the shoes on and joined A.J. She helped him wash off the coolers and haul them inside.

"Running a church like this is a big operation, huh?"

"I don't run it." A.J. chuckled. "But I know what you mean. It takes a lot of people working together. I do a little here with the youth group. Other people teach classes or lead singing or balance the books. It's like a machine ... or a body."

"A body?" What a strange metaphor.

"You know, from 1 Corinthians? All the different people of the church make up the different body parts. Like an ear or a foot or ..." He shook his head. "I sound a little crazy. I can't say it as well as Paul did."

"No, no." Madeleine laughed. "It sounds familiar now. Each person brings something different to the table."

"Yes! Exactly." A.J. grinned, holding her gaze a little longer than strictly necessary. Madeleine's stomach flipped. Again. Get it together, Madeleine! Just friends. Just friends.

Madeleine repeated the words in her head as they walked out to her car. Just friends. And still as she plugged her phone into her car charger. Just friends. And as she typed their destination into her phone. Just friends.

"Where are we headed?"

"Just friends—I mean ... just the friendly neighborhood hardware store." Madeleine smiled, hoping her quick save was convincing.

"You don't need to go to some fancy schmancy art store?"

"Nope. We're buying regular old latex paint and some other basic supplies we can find anywhere. I'll pull out some fancy schmancy paint brushes later when I'm adding the detail."

"Oh, good. I was beginning to question whether or not you're a real artist."

Madeleine laughed. "Oh, don't worry. I have plenty of expensive materials. Art school was not cheap. I mean, I had a good scholarship, but there's still paint and paper and brushes and all the random stuff you're supposed to have to be a real artist. I just hope it was all worth it."

"I'm sure it was." A.J. scratched the back of his neck. "I, uh, I saw your portfolio online."

"Really?" Her website was accessible to everyone, of course, but she hadn't expected A.J. to be interested in her work.

"Really. It was good. You're very talented."

Madeleine was glad she was focusing ahead on the road and not on A.J.'s face. She knew she wasn't bad. Her grades and the compliments she'd gotten along the way proved as much. But art was such a subjective thing, her heart thrilled to hear that A.J. liked her work.

"Thanks. Anything in particular you liked?" She added quickly, "Not that I'm fishing for compliments. I just like to know what sticks out to people."

"You can fish for compliments. I'm happy to oblige." A.J. thought for a moment. "There was one—an oil painting, I think —of a woman. She reminded me of you."

"That's my mother. She didn't care for that one, said it was too sad.

That's why it's for sale."

"She did seem a little sad, yes. But it was really interesting. It was as if I could see inside of her, feel what she's feeling."

Madeleine drove in silence for a while. Her mother had been sad for a long time. Too long. All because of her father and this tiny town. This lovely little place that would always be home, no matter how long they'd been away. If only … if only they could move on and forget all of the pain and sorrow of the past. Leave it there where it belonged. This sadness and bitterness simply made everyone miserable. But she struggled to remember what life was like before.

"Thanks. For the compliments. I'm really glad you liked it." Madeleine gave a small smile.

Half an hour later, they arrived at the hardware store. A.J. pushed the shopping cart as Madeleine pulled supplies off the shelf. A roll of tape, a small can of primer, a long drop cloth, a roller brush, and a bottle of paint extender all went into the cart. She quickly picked out cans of yellow, red, white, and black paint and walked around the store with A.J. as they waited for a can of blue to be mixed.

"That was really fast," said A.J. "I guess you've done this before."

"A few times. Honestly, at first it was weird picking out paint at a hardware store instead of an art store. I was so used to getting tiny tubes of expensive paint and tiny expensive paint brushes. Working on a large scale can be a lot more fun sometimes. It's a little messier and freer than a small painting. A little more complicated, too."

"How's that?" A.J. asked.

"Well, any mistakes you make could get amplified. And you have to make sure a mural looks good close up and far away. Most paintings are a hot mess when you get up really close."

"Ha! That's so true. Like pointillism or impressionism, you have to be far away to really understand what's going on."

"I'm impressed." Apparently, she wasn't the only art nerd.

"Hey, I had to take art appreciation just like everybody else," A.J. said. "But I also happened to enjoy taking it."

"Really." Madeleine nodded. "You are full of surprises, A.J. Young."

They wandered the aisles, toying around with random objects. A lampshade here, a door knocker there. Madeleine inhaled deeply the smell of wood and potting soil and floor varnish, or whatever scents made hardware stores smell so good.

"Coming here always reminds me of my dad." A.J.'s gaze shot to Madeleine, an apology in his eyes, as if only now remembering she'd grown up without a father. "Sorry, I didn't …"

"It's okay. Tell me about your dad."

"Well, he's actually not very good at building things or fixing things—he's much better in front of a computer—but he used to get these wild hairs and bring me to the hardware store to build a treehouse or fix a leaky pipe." A.J. picked up a small brush and stuck it under his nose like a mustache. "Son," he said in a deep, ridiculous voice. "There's nothing like a job well done. You can count on that, son."

"Does your dad really sound that way? Like, if I stole your cell phone and called your dad, he would sound that way?"

"Son, is that you? Son?" A.J. held the phone in one hand and the brush in another, still using the silly voice.

Laughing with A.J. was so good. So what if they couldn't be more than friends? Spending time with him as a friend was more than enough.

"Uh, ma'am, your paint is ready." Madeleine hadn't seen the store employee approach them. Apparently, A.J. hadn't either, because he fumbled the paintbrush before hastily returning it to the shelf.

"Thanks. We'll be right there," Madeleine said, trying her best not to laugh in the man's face.

Once she'd gotten her giggles out and paid for her cartload, Madeleine and A.J. started back to Shady Springs.

"Wait! Pull over here!" A.J. pointed wildly to the parking lot of a hair salon and tattoo parlor.

"Okay. Why?" Madeleine hastily obeyed, not sure what could have caused this sudden emergency.

"Shave ice!" A.J. explained, still pointing and smiling broadly.

Madeleine followed the direction of his finger and saw a tiny snow cone stand. A modest line of people waited under sunshades while others ate their frozen treats at nearby picnic tables. Madeleine pulled up as close to the stand as she could and parked the car.

"C'mon!" A.J. said. "You'll love it, I promise."

"Yeah, I've had snow cones before."

"These are the best, trust me." A.J. came around to Madeleine's side of the car and opened the door for her. She would've thought it was a chivalrous gesture if he didn't immediately push her toward the line.

As with most snow cone stands, the list of flavors was massive, but Madeleine almost always ordered peach or strawberry.

"Whatever you get, make sure to add cream. It's totally worth it. And I'm paying, since I'm the one who made us stop." A.J. dismissed her objections with a wave of his hand. "No, no. I insist."

Madeleine wanted to resist the kind offer more strongly, but she couldn't deny she was low on funds and shouldn't be splurging on sweets. She stepped up to the window. "I'll have a small peach with cream."

"And a medium strawberry mango with cream," A.J. added, handing over a few dollar bills.

Madeleine turned around to watch the other happy customers —the place had a loyal following—but she didn't miss the clink of change as

A.J. dropped some quarters in the tip jar. Madeleine liked that. Treating food servers well was a sign of good character.

By the time their snow cones were ready, Madeleine had really gotten excited. A.J.'s enthusiasm was contagious. She took one small taste and was immediately overwhelmed. The ice was smooth and soft as snow. The syrup tasted like the freshest peach cobbler she'd ever eaten. And the cream sent the whole flavor experience over the top.

"This is amazing," Madeleine confessed between bites. "You were completely right."

"I always come here when I'm in town during the summer. The owners are really nice, too. Frank and Betty. Although it's usually students working the booths. They have another location closer to downtown."

"You come here so often, you know the owners?" Madeleine asked. "That's a lot of snow cones."

"Technically, they're not snow cones. They're Hawaiian-style shave ice." A.J. waved his spoon at her.

"Shaved ice. I thought they were the same." No matter, they were delicious either way.

"No 'd.' Just shave ice." He pointed to the sign. "Shave ice."

"Very good, Miss Mullins." A.J. nodded at her in mock condescension.

Madeleine stuck out her tongue at him for being so obnoxious. "Is my tongue bright orange?"

"Yeah, is mine bright red?" A.J. stuck out his tongue, too.

"Yes. But this is totally worth it." Madeleine shoved another mouthful in to emphasize her point.

"It is. I'd look ridiculous for the sake of shave ice anytime," A.J. said, his own mouth full.

"What's your excuse the rest of the time?" Madeleine couldn't resist a good jab. Teasing was a habit she'd picked up from her Uncle George.

"Ha. ha." A.J. playfully punched her shoulder. "You think I look ridiculous?"

"No," Madeleine answered before her brain caught up and she could stop herself. "I don't think you look ridiculous at all." That was quite the understatement.

"Yeah? I don't think you look ridiculous either."

In that moment, as their eyes locked, Madeleine knew A.J. liked her just as much as she liked him. Whatever reservations he and Nancy Jones might have about him dating a girl who wasn't a Christian, he clearly experienced the same magnetic attraction Madeleine had from the moment she laid eyes on him. Madeleine's cheeks warmed, and she diverted her attention back to her shave ice. She couldn't help but smile as she finished off her—still incredibly delicious—dessert.

12

*N*othing could be better than a day spent on the water followed by some amazing shave ice. And the company wasn't too bad, either. A.J. had enjoyed Madeleine's presence on the trip, even if it only meant an extra pair of hands to pass out lunches and an extra set of eyes to keep the kids in line. But, beyond that, their time together had solidified their growing friendship. He hadn't had so much fun with a woman in a long time.

"Thanks again for coming along with us this morning. I'm glad you could make it."

"Me, too. I hadn't been canoeing in years, and I ended up liking it more than I remembered, despite ... everything." She grimaced as she clenched the steering wheel.

Everything, meaning Mitchell and the boys tipping their canoe. Something A.J. fully expected to happen every time he went out on the river. In fact, he'd been pretty impressed at how well the guys had flipped the boat, which was a thing of beauty, really. Madeleine obviously did not share his admiration of their canoe-flipping prowess, but she appeared to have gotten over it.

"I'm glad you talked to Mitchell. Water under the bridge,

now. Ha, get it? Water?" He searched her eyes for a hint of amusement.

"Right, water." Her gaze remained fixed on the road. Obviously, Madeleine didn't think the joke was as funny as A.J. did. Or maybe her mind was on other things. "It's just ... he still didn't apologize. Or even acknowledge that I was being the bigger person by going over there and talking to him. All he said was Uh, yeah. Thanks." The last part was said in a deep, stupid-sounding voice, meant to sound like Mitchell, apparently. Maybe Madeleine hadn't quite gotten over it.

"I know that it upset you, but they're just kids. Those boys are used to roughhousing with me, and they got carried away."

"Well, they shouldn't have."

"Yes, you're completely right. And I'm sorry about your shoe—"

"It's not about the shoe."

"Well then, I don't understand." Heat rose to A.J.'s cheeks. "All they did was tip the canoe. We got a little wet. That's why we wore swimsuits."

"Really? I thought it was very immature of them. Besides, all Mitchell had to do was say he was sorry."

He didn't like getting flustered. In fact, A.J.'s calm demeanor was a point of pride. He was the level-headed teacher. Mr. Cool-as-a-Cucumber. He was the guy people wanted in an emergency, and this woman had managed to fluster him. "Maybe you're being a little too sensitive."

As soon as the words left A.J.'s mouth, the air in the car got about ten degrees cooler.

"Too sensitive?" Madeleine's voice was quiet but icy. A.J. wished he could take back what he'd said, but it was too late.

"So, I'm just being too emotional, too sensitive, too weak and feminine, probably." She glared at the road ahead.

Where was this coming from? A.J. was not prepared for this battle. He knew he should apologize. At the very least, he should keep his mouth shut. But A.J. had never been very good at keeping his mouth shut.

"I didn't mean to say that. I didn't mean any of that."

"Well, what did you mean?" Her voice grew a little louder.

A.J. was losing control of the conversation. He wasn't completely sure he'd ever had any control. The argument was about gender now? Or maybe feelings? Subjects that required a certain level of finesse, which A.J. simply did not possess. "Those are your words, not mine. Listen, I—"

"Oh, listen up while the man explains to the weak, sensitive woman," she interrupted, her words flying out faster and angrier. The car accelerated to match her frustration.

"It's not like that, Madeleine. Will you slow down for a second?"

Madeleine checked the speedometer and released some pressure on the gas pedal. A.J. breathed a little easier. He had obviously hit a button by calling Madeleine sensitive. He wished that button had come with a bright red sign.

"Why won't you take my side? Why couldn't Mitchell just apologize?" She sounded a little hurt.

"I didn't take any sides." Why wouldn't Madeleine calm down and listen to him? "Why can't you let this go? It wasn't a big deal. You're making it so much worse than it has to be."

Madeleine squinted and adjusted the rearview mirror. A.J. squirmed in his seat while he waited for her to say something.

"I didn't realize you had such a low opinion of me, A.J. That you think I'm too sensitive and too immature." She took a deep breath. "If this is how things are going to be with you, maybe we should stop spending time together."

The words hit A.J. like a blow to the chest. "If that's what you really want," he said quietly.

"I think it is."

"Okay, then."

And that was that. They drove the next twenty minutes in

total silence. A.J. closed his eyes, trying to rack his brain for a way to save the conversation. A way to save their friendship, but he couldn't.

Maybe this was for the best. Sam had told him to guard his heart, and closing himself off to Madeleine would certainly solve that problem. But for some reason, even though he was angry at her, his heart still tugged toward the woman in the car with him. He wanted to fix this, to patch things up with Madeleine, but he didn't want to make the situation worse than it already was. His words only dug him into a deeper and deeper hole. Madeleine pulled the car into the church parking lot slowly and dropped A.J. off right next to his pickup truck. A.J. turned to say something, anything, to Madeleine, but his mouth opened and closed without any sound. The words just wouldn't come. His heart breaking, A.J. stepped out of the car and left.

* * *

"Come on, Maddy. It'll be fun." Uncle George poked her in the shoulder.

Maddy rolled her eyes and continued to stare out the window. She couldn't remember exactly how her uncle had managed to talk her into this trip, but somehow, she'd ended up here. Where was here? They were at least an hour away from Shady Springs and another half hour away from the run-down cabin where they'd rented a canoe. Now she sat in a rusted old pickup that stank of mildew and tobacco.

When the truck finally stopped, they all jumped out, and Maddy watched George and the man from the rental place unload their boat. Maddy tried to listen to the instructions, but they washed over her, much like a lot of things did nowadays.

Maddy was trying to focus in school, for Mom's sake, but this year had been hard. Seventh grade would have been difficult enough without starting over in a new town. To top it all off, she hadn't heard from her dad in almost a year. He'd called a few times after he left, to check in on her. Each time they talked, it was harder and harder. Not just to keep the hurt out of her voice. But also to heal her broken heart after they hung up. And then he stopped calling.

Mom was stressed, too. She hadn't worked full-time since Maddy was born, but she'd taken a position as a surgery nurse at a large hospital. Her job was demanding, and she came home exhausted every night. Well, not every night. Some nights she was off, and they would watch movies together or play games. But neither of them was a lot of fun to hang out with. And now her mom was talking about going back to school, which would mean more busy nights.

Maddy loved her mother. They were together in this. Whatever this was. The abandonment club. The saddest, loneliest club ever. Attendance at weekly cry sessions was mandatory. Dues to be paid in broken hearts. Dad left both of them, and they were both hurting. No one else understood. Not Aunt Clara or Uncle George. Not the school counselor. No one.

Clara and George had tried to help, inviting her out to Shady Springs for a few weeks this summer. Mom wanted to come, but she couldn't get off work that long. So, she'd dropped Maddy off and would pick Maddy up again, staying for a couple days.

Each time Sunday rolled around, Clara and George would invite Maddy to come to church with them. And each time, Maddy politely refused. They didn't push her, although Maddy felt guilty when she saw the disappointment in their eyes. Just not guilty enough to actually go with them.

Uncle George had insisted time in the canoe would be good for her. Fresh air, blah, blah, blah, and whatever else he thought teenage girls needed. So Maddy had agreed to go with him, if only to get him off her back.

She had to admit, the water was beautiful. Birds chirped and leaves rustled in the wind. Kelly, emerald, and lime green filtered through the trees and reflected in the river. Maddy let her fingers dangle in the water, which was cool to the touch, despite the ninety-degree weather.

For a long time, George let them float slowly, not breaking the peaceful quiet. "I know you're angry."

"Really? I wonder why that is?" No duh.

"Your dad may have left, but I didn't. And Clara didn't. We're still here. We always will be."

"Lucky me." Maddy bit her lip. She hadn't meant for that to come out. The harsh words didn't match the love she had for Uncle George and Aunt Clara. But they did match the black, oozing wound festering in her heart. Maddy and her uncle floated in tense silence for a few minutes.

"It's not your fault," he said.

"What's that supposed to mean?" Her words were biting and defensive. "I just want you to know, it's not your fault."

"Why does everyone assume I think it's my fault?" She'd heard the same thing from her counselor and from all of the sad books her teacher recommended.

"It's a normal thing for children to think."

"I'm thirteen." Why did everyone treat her like a child but expect her to cope like an adult?

George pushed his oar through the water, maneuvering their canoe to the middle of the river before sliding the oar into his lap. "Your father is sick. Not in a way you can see from the outside, but on the inside. His mind and his heart are sick. It had nothing to do with you, or even your mother."

"Mom says he's been drinking instead of dealing with life." Her voice was almost a whisper. Maddy turned to look at Uncle George, squinting in the bright sunlight.

"I used to know Henry back in high school. He was older, but everyone knew who he was. He still has that same smile, the one all the girls like." George shook his head. "He could've been one of those cruel, popular boys—we had a few of those at our school—but Henry was always nice. Everyone liked him." George rubbed the back of his neck, squinting at Maddy. "I guess what I'm trying to say is, I think he's going to be okay. I think that after he works through all this stuff, he's going to come out all right. Because your dad is one of the good guys. He has a good heart."

"How long before he works through it?" Maddy wasn't sure she could wait much longer. The distance from her father still hurt, like someone had wrenched out part of her body and taken it away.

"I don't know, Maddy. I wish I knew."

They floated for another half an hour in quiet, Maddy helping Uncle George as much as she could with steering the canoe. They kept the boat steady but didn't force it to go any faster than necessary, keeping time with the river. Maddy stretched and gazed up at the brilliant blue sky above her.

"I miss him, too, you know," Uncle George said. "Henry was one of my best friends."

Maddy had never thought about that before, but her parents must have best friends, too. They were people, after all. Aunt Clara was probably Mom's best friend. But who were Dad's friends? Did he have any close friends anymore?

"Thanks, Uncle George." She sighed. "I'm sorry I've been such a brat lately."

"Comes with the territory. I could be a brat, too, when I was your age."

"I doubt that."

"Yeah, I was pretty good most of the time."

"Sounds more like it." Maddy laughed, imagining a teenage Uncle George.

He was such a nerd now; he was probably even worse in junior high. "You're pretty good, too, Maddy."

A sense of calm sank into Madeleine's heart. She hadn't talked or smiled this much in a while. She wanted her dad back, more than anything else in the world. But George wasn't so bad.

"Thanks, Uncle George." She gave a small smile. "You were right, this is nice."

"Yeah. It is."

Maddy tried her hardest to enjoy the rest of the day and didn't even correct the man who called Uncle George her father while collecting their canoes. Despite the bitterness, she was lucky to have Clara and George, and she spent the rest of the week acting like she was happy until she thought it might actually be true.

13

On Tuesday morning, Madeleine woke up with sore arms. The combination of rowing down the river Monday morning and washing the wall for her mural Monday evening left her muscles aching. Perhaps she'd scrubbed the walls a little too hard last night. Her mom called it anger cleaning, and it was something at which they both excelled. Madeleine's college roommate always joked that Madeleine's side of the room was neatest right before she had a big project due. Any kind of stress always made her itch to clean or exercise.

On this particular morning, Madeleine decided to spend the rest of her pent-up energy jogging and enjoying the sunshine before a predicted rainstorm moved in. She threw on some workout clothes— noting that she was almost out of clean clothes—gulped down a glass of water, scribbled a note for Clara, and headed outside.

The morning air was thick with the threat of rain but cool, nevertheless. Madeleine briskly walked for a block before picking up the pace, relishing the familiar slap-slap-slap as her tennis shoes hit the pavement. A few streets away from Clara's house was the school, and a few more blocks from that was an expansive cattle pasture Madeleine liked to use as her halfway point.

As houses and trees and azalea bushes flew past, Madeleine's mind returned to the events of yesterday. A.J.'s laughter echoing through the river canyon, his red hair practically glowing in the sunshine, the way his arms pushed the canoe effortlessly through the water. Like a handful of smooth river rocks, Madeleine massaged and polished the memories in her mind, turning them over and over. Sweetest and most cherished of all was the memory of A.J. staring at her, a mirror of her inexplicable attraction toward him. The same draw, the same pull that tugged her heart toward his was reflected on his face.

But the memory that loomed over all the others, still jagged and rough no matter how many times she relived it, was the fight and silent car drive that ended her time with A.J. yesterday. Her anger had lessened with the new day, but his words had pierced her, and the wound had not yet healed.

Madeleine's footsteps fell faster and faster as A.J.'s voice echoed in her head. Too sensitive. Such a male thing to say. As if by being in touch with her emotions, she was weak. How dare he. What a jerk. What a—

Madeleine came to an abrupt stop at the fence around the cattle pasture. She caught her breath in bursts, leaning against the rails for support. She couldn't keep on like this. A.J. was supposed to be a friend, nothing more. Why did his opinion of her matter so much? If she was going to make it back to Kansas City with her heart still intact, she needed to reign things in. Focus on the mural and then get out of here.

Shaking her head, as if that would erase the thoughts of A.J., Madeleine refocused. Next time I see A.J., I will be cool and calm and detached. She stretched her neck and shoulders, then returned to Aunt Clara's house where her work and reality would be waiting for her.

"I'm back from my jog," Madeleine called out as she closed the side door and trudged up the stairs.

She didn't wait to hear a response before turning on the shower. Today was going to be busy. She hoped to prime the wall for painting and start sketching outlines. Even though Sam hadn't approved a final version of the mural, she could get started with the prep work.

After showering and dressing—she definitely needed to wash some clothes tonight—Madeleine grabbed a bite to eat in the kitchen. Usually,

Clara had something out for breakfast. Muffins, eggs, bacon, or cereal at the very least. But Madeleine found the countertop completely bare. There wasn't any coffee in the coffee pot or even any dirty dishes in the sink. I guess my jog went a little late. I should be better about getting up in the morning … or maybe Aunt Clara is sleeping in.

Madeleine crept up to Clara's room and pressed her ear against the door. A soft snore resonated from inside. Better not disturb her. Poor thing must be worn out from the end of the school year.

Madeleine snuck across the hall into her bedroom to grab her things. Not that her volume really mattered. She'd been loud as an elephant crashing around the house all morning and hadn't woken her aunt yet.

All of her paint was over at the church building, so Madeleine was able to fit everything she needed into one bag. Downstairs, she grabbed a granola bar and a banana. The weather was still nice, and her bag so light, she decided to walk.

Once inside, Madeleine pulled out the drop cloth and some painter's tape to protect the floor from any splatters. She would be in big trouble if she ruined the pristine carpet in the brand-new children's wing. The night before, Madeleine had washed the wall with soapy water and some rags from the supply closet. The closet was super creepy and probably filled with spiders, so she'd gone ahead and pulled out a ladder while she was in there so she wouldn't have to return later. Now, with the floors covered and all of her painting accoutrements at the ready, she opened the can of primer and got to work.

There was something beautiful and frightening about a blank, white space. So much potential could be either good or bad. A blank canvas could give way to a masterpiece or a mistake, or worse, a mediocre piece of art.

By the end of the morning, the wall would be prepared for Madeleine's mural. But what was Madeleine being prepared for? She'd only been in Arkansas a few days, but Shady Springs was working under her skin, getting to her. If she stayed here too long, would she be primed for heartbreak?

Working out her sore muscles felt good at first, but by the time she was finished priming the wall, Madeleine was more than ready for a break. The clock on her phone read noon, so she headed to Aunt Clara's house for some lunch.

Clara was a good cook, and she shared Madeleine's taste for the exotic. Much more than Madeleine's mother. Clara could usually be counted on for something delicious and unexpected. Would it be tikka masala today? Or maybe a mint and berry salad or perhaps some leftover tomato gazpacho from last night with a gouda and pesto panini?

Clouds gathered in the sky for the promised storm. Madeleine was glad the rain hadn't started yet, as she'd completely forgotten to bring an umbrella. She was only about halfway when a drop of water hit her on the nose. Another on her right arm. Two more on her left arm. Madeleine quickened her pace, speed-walking and feeling more than a little ridiculous. And then, without further warning, the storm broke, and Madeleine was completely drenched. She ran, trying not to slip on the slick sidewalks, racing through the neighborhood for the second time that day.

She was in such a hurry she almost didn't notice the extra car parked outside, which would have been impossible to miss in any other circumstance, being a bright yellow two-seater. Whoever owned that vehicle certainly wasn't Clara. Madeleine rushed inside, hoping her aunt's visitor didn't mind soaking wet girls coming in and interrupting lunch.

Sitting at the kitchen table was quite easily the most beautiful woman Madeleine had ever seen. She appeared to be in her late thirties with short, dark hair and caramel skin. She gave Madeleine a warm smile that reminded her of chicken noodle soup. Although maybe the smell of chicken soup was actually what made her think of that.

"Madeleine, this is Julie Ortega. She's one of my dear friends from church and has come to visit this widow in her affliction." Next to Julie, Clara was a colorless figure. Still wearing her pajamas and a bathrobe, her hair up in a very messy bun, Clara obviously had not had a good morning.

"Are you sick?" Madeleine started to give her aunt a hug but held back. A wet hug from her would do more harm than good.

"It's just my annual sick day. No worries." Clara smiled gamely but looked all the more pathetic for her bravery.

"Every year, Clara comes down with a cold after school lets out," Julie said. "And every year I bring her my abuelita's soup. It's a family recipe—works like a charm."

"It's true. Every year it heals me." Clara noisily sipped a spoonful of soup to emphasize her point. To Julie she said, "I wish you would share the recipe, but then I wouldn't get the pleasure of your company."

"I'm happy to make it for you." Julie patted her hand, then lifted her gaze to Madeleine again. "You're soaking wet! You must've gotten caught in the rainstorm."

"I did. Let me change, and I'll join you." Madeleine slipped off her wet shoes and socks and climbed the stairs to her room.

"Hurry up. If you stay in those wet clothes too long, you'll end up just like me," Clara called after her.

Madeleine pulled on her very last set of clothes, a pair of sweatpants and a T-shirt, and marched down the stairs with her full laundry basket. "Mind if I do some laundry?" she asked as she walked through the kitchen on her way to the laundry room. Then, as an afterthought, she said, "I could do yours, too, if you have any."

"That's very kind of you. See what I have in the laundry basket and throw it in with yours." Clara punctuated her words with three loud sneezes in her tissue.

Madeleine was glad she'd thought to offer her help, even if it did mean an extra trip upstairs. She'd been absent all morning while Clara was sick and helpless. Madeleine had thought she knew everything about her aunt, but this Julie lady was showing her there were plenty of things she didn't know about Aunt Clara. Things her friends at church knew, like annual illnesses and favorite soups.

Madeleine had mixed emotions about this. Obviously, she was glad Aunt Clara had friends to take care of her when her family was far away. Madeleine didn't want her aunt to be lonely or helpless. But there were certain things Madeleine had thought only family could provide. In a way, Madeleine had been replaced by Aunt Clara's church. Her "church family" as she always called them.

Madeleine dropped her clothes into the washing machine before dutifully returning upstairs. An investigation of the closet showed she did, indeed, have some clothes to add to Madeleine's large pile of dirty laundry. As she hauled out the laundry baskets, Madeleine paused at George's side of the closet.

Aunt Clara had long ago sold or given away most of Uncle George's belongings. She'd only kept the items she couldn't bear to part with. The things that still held George's essence. His favorite tie. His camping gear. His favorite books. A couple shirts and a blazer that held some unknown significance to Clara. A pair of shoes that must remind her of something.

Madeleine reached for the sleeve of the blazer and held it up to her nose. Of course, the blazer had been sitting in the closet for four years, so it didn't smell anything like Uncle George. The reminder that he was gone—really gone—and had been gone a long time brought sudden tears to her eyes. Madeleine wiped her face with her sleeve and tried to force down the lump in her throat. She sat on Aunt Clara's bed. Her gaze drifted over the family pictures on the dresser. In a way, she'd lost two fathers.

Madeleine read once that a divorce was harder than a death. Having lost people to both, Madeleine decided they were both terrible. But there was a comfort she found in poring over the pictures of George, brilliant and passionate and very much alive, that she never found in memories of her father. His leaving had worked backward to tarnish every memory of him until they were all sour.

Clara always said two things got her through the death of George. The first was the hope of heaven. She believed one day, everyone who followed God would be reunited to live together with Him forever. Madeleine desperately wanted that to be true. Losing her uncle had been wrong. Against everything that was natural. Sitting there on Aunt Clara's bed, Madeleine searched inside herself. A part of her, something deep inside, was neither bone nor skin nor blood but … soul. Didn't that part of her feel immortal? Wasn't her soul meant to go on forever?

The second thing was the love of the church. Madeleine had experienced some of that with Sam and the kids in the youth group. And with A.J. … before their fight. She wished everyone in the church was loving and kind, but Madeleine knew from experience that wasn't true. She stood and picked up the laundry hampers again. Downstairs, Julie and Clara were giggling over something.

Julie seemed like a good-hearted person. And if she had been taking care of Clara all this time, Madeleine owed it to her to be friendly in return. Once Madeleine had sorted all the clothes and started the first load, she joined Julie and Clara at the kitchen table.

"Would you like some soup? Let me get some for you." Before Madeleine could protest, Julie was across the kitchen with a ladle and a bowl.

"Thank you, Julie." Madeleine inhaled the steam of the fragrant bowl before her. "Mmm, this is amazing."

"See? I told you." Clara smiled and patted Julie's knee. "Julie sure makes a mean chicken soup."

Madeleine wasn't sure exactly what was in the soup, except for black beans, zucchini, onions, and chicken. There was definitely some type of pepper because a smoky spiciness kicked in a couple seconds after her first sip. Madeleine coughed a little and wiped her nose. The soup could really clear out the sinuses. No wonder Aunt Clara liked it for colds.

"So, Julie, how long have you lived in Shady Springs?" Madeleine took a giant gulp of water.

"Only a few years. I moved here from Dallas for work."

"Oh? What do you do?" And why would anyone ever move from a bustling metropolis like Dallas, Texas to tiny Shady Springs, Arkansas?

"I run a bridal shop in Northwest Arkansas. MK Lambert." Julie said it like it was no big deal, but MK Lambert was a super classy, appointment-only bridal store.

"For real? I love their dresses!"

"Since when are you in the market for a wedding dress?" Aunt Clara laughed but stopped when she saw how seriously Madeleine and Julie stared back at her.

"Um, since always. Just because I'm not engaged doesn't mean I can't admire wedding dresses. Besides, I need to know what kind of dress I like before I get married. These things take time."

"She's right. Single women are perfectly entitled to dream

about their weddings. I know I sure have." A wistful look filled Julie's eyes.

"You're single, too? But you're so ..." Madeleine struggled for the words. She wouldn't be so rude as to comment on Julie's physical appearance only minutes after meeting her for the first time.

"Drop dead gorgeous?" Aunt Clara happily filled in the exact thing Madeleine was thinking.

"Ah, you think so, but this body and I have had many struggles."

Madeleine didn't want to pry, but she waited and hoped Julie would continue.

"Before I came here, for many years, I struggled with an eating disorder. My whole life I was told how beautiful I was and how my looks would be my ticket to success. I was terrified of becoming fat or old and terrified of becoming a slave to my body, so I took control in the only way I knew how." Julie relayed the facts of her story without tears or even a shadow of sadness. She'd clearly come a long way since the days of her eating disorder.

"I'm so sorry. How did you get better?" Madeleine had judged Julie too harshly before she knew anything about her.

"Jesus." Julie smiled, and a glow lit up her face as she clarified. "I grew up Catholic but not really believing in God. When a friend took me with her to church, my whole life changed. It didn't happen overnight. There was a lot of therapy and hard work, but none of that would have changed anything if I didn't believe my worth is found in Jesus. I believe God will always love me, no matter my outward appearance, no matter how many mistakes I make."

"He will. I am so thankful for that love, too." Aunt Clara patted Julie's hand softly. Madeleine could tell they'd had many conversations about Julie's struggle.

"You know, the church in Shady Springs has been a lifeline

for me. Before I became a Christian, all of my relationships were dysfunctional because of my hatred for my body and myself. I'm grateful for Clara and all of my friends here." Julie laughed. "And they trust me enough to put me in charge of the food ministry."

"You are so organized and such a good cook. We'd be crazy not to." Aunt Clara took another appreciative sip of her soup.

"God has redeemed everything for me, including food." Julie smiled gently at Madeleine. She couldn't tell if Julie knew everything about her history with the church. Surely, Aunt Clara had talked to her about it. Despite her usual skepticism, Madeleine believed Julie was speaking from her heart.

As the rain outside died down, Julie poured the extra soup in some plastic containers and packed away her slow cooker. Madeleine moved the first load of laundry into the dryer, being careful to hang up the more delicate of Aunt Clara's blouses, and started on the next load. Julie said her goodbyes, and Aunt Clara begged leave to rest in her bedroom.

With nothing to do but wait on the laundry, Madeleine pulled out Sam's Bible once again. What could it hurt to read a little more?

"Divorce" read the first heading in chapter nineteen. Madeleine rolled her eyes, but the truth was she actually agreed with everything Jesus had to say. Madeleine blamed her parents' separation for a lot of the pain in her life. Divorce was not something to be taken lightly.

She knew when she finally started dating someone, really and seriously dating, she would do it with the utmost caution. Madeleine never wanted to make the same mistakes her parents had made. That's why she'd only ever been on a handful of dates. So far, she hadn't found anyone who measured up.

When the last load of laundry was dry and all the clothes were folded, Madeleine headed to the church building to work on the mural. She checked on Aunt Clara before she left and found her sitting in bed reading. She looked a little better after her nap, but Madeleine hoped not to work too long so she could be around to help if her aunt needed anything.

Now that the wall was primed and dried, Madeleine started to mark out a grid, halving the space in two, then splitting those halves into four, and so on. When she finished, each square on the wall would correspond to a square on her sketch. Then, she would transcribe the drawing from her paper to the wall.

The job was not glamorous, but it was simple. Just measure and draw lines. While she worked, her mind wandered. Madeleine had always thought she would decide what she believed about God and religion when she became an adult. Somewhere between getting married and having kids. But the more she read about Jesus, the more she heard a calling. A little voice asking, Why not? Why not right now?

What held her back, what always held her back, was Nancy Jones. Not only her, but others like her, too. People who claimed to love everybody but ended up treating everyone else around them like dirt. Hypocrites.

But didn't Jesus hate hypocrisy, too? Wasn't He always praising the simple people? The needy. The children. The uneducated. Why, then, was the church so broken? Why were Christians so hateful sometimes?

That evening, Madeleine reheated some soup in the microwave. She arranged the bowl, a few crackers, and a mug of tea on a tray and carried it upstairs to Aunt Clara's room.

"Dinner in bed?" Madeleine knocked gently on the door before pushing it open.

"Oh, that's so sweet of you." Clara sat straighter and lowered her reading glasses. She was looking better but was clearly ready to return to sleep soon.

"I brought you some more of Julie's chicken soup. Hope you're not sick of it."

"No, not at all. That's very kind." Aunt Clara accepted the

tray from Madeleine and placed it over her legs. "Would you like to join me? Heat some up for yourself and we'll have a picnic in bed."

"Are you sure? I don't want to wear you out."

"No, no. I could use the conversation. I'm already getting a little stir crazy."

Madeleine returned a few minutes later with her own piping hot bowl and sat at the foot of the bed facing her aunt.

"So, what did you do all day? I'm sorry I've been out of commission today. I promise I'll be much better tomorrow." Clara basked in the warm steam rising from her bowl and smiled contentedly.

"No, I'm sorry." Madeleine grimaced. "I should've been around to take care of you."

"Oh, I'm pretty used to taking care of myself. What do you think I do while you're home in Kansas City?"

"Take care of yourself, I guess. And you have Julie to take care of you." Madeleine tried not to let the touch of jealousy she still had come out in her voice. She had to accept that Julie could love her aunt, too.

"Yes, Julie. She's a real sweetheart." Aunt Clara slurped loudly. "And a good cook to boot."

"I can't believe all the stuff she's been through."

"Sure you can."

"Pardon?" The comment was so sudden and brazen Madeleine almost choked on her soup.

"You can believe what she's been through because we've all been through stuff. You've been through stuff. I've been through stuff." Clara stopped to blow her nose. "None of us is squeaky clean. Life leaves wounds. Whether or not you choose to let God heal them is another thing." Aunt Clara was even less filtered than usual in her speech. Maybe she was under the influence of the cold—or the cold medicine—but Madeleine kind of liked her aunt's brutal honesty tonight.

"I guess that's what I mean. I can't believe someone so beautiful and well-adjusted went through such a hard time."

"She did. I agree, it is amazing. But she's not all that special. Everyone I know at that little church comes to Jesus broken. We all have baggage. Some of it shows more clearly on the outside than others. But we all need Jesus. You do, too, if you'd admit it."

Madeleine ducked her head. She desperately wanted to ask Aunt Clara all of the questions she had about Jesus and the church, but she was terrified of the pressure that would add. She knew the thing Aunt Clara wanted most in the world was for her and her mother to return to church. If she even told her aunt she was reading the Bible, let alone had real questions about everything, that would give Aunt Clara a seed of hope. And Madeleine would rather keep everything bottled up inside than kill that hope and disappoint her aunt.

A subject change was in order. Thankfully, Aunt Clara was more than happy to talk about the book she was reading, and they spent the rest of their dinner in happy conversation. Madeleine cleaned up the dishes afterward and sent her aunt off to sleep, hopeful that tomorrow would bring more answers than questions.

* * *

Mom zipped Maddy's black dress and latched the little hook in the back. What was the point of those hooks anyway? In case the zipper broke? Seemed like it wouldn't do a whole lot of good. She asked her mother.

"It's to take the stress off the zipper. So the zipper doesn't have to do all the work. It helps keep everything in good condition a little longer."

Stress. There had been a lot of stress lately. Late night phone calls. Long trips from Kansas City to Shady Springs. Cards and flowers. Then funeral arrangements. And more cards and flowers. Maddy didn't much care for flowers right now.

"Let's go. We don't want your aunt to be alone when the visitation starts." They hadn't given Aunt Clara much alone time since Uncle George got sick.

Between their trips to Shady Springs, days spent in the hospital and doctors' offices, and the church ladies' visits with casseroles and condolences, Aunt Clara probably hadn't had a moment's peace in a year. Although, now that Uncle George was gone, Aunt Clara would have too much time alone. Already the rooms carried an unnatural stillness, as if even the house itself knew he was gone.

Maddy dutifully stood with her aunt and mother as people from the church and the community streamed by, offering empty words meant to bring comfort. To an observer, Maddy imagined they resembled three crows in a line, stooped and dark. People had always commented on how much they all looked alike. How much more today in their matching black dresses and matching sorrowful faces.

Beside her, Gramma and Grandpa Hodges held hands. They leaned into each other like two sides of a triangle each holding the other upright. Gramma saw Maddy glancing her way and offered a teary smile.

On the other side of the casket, Uncle George's family stood in their own black clothes and sad faces. Once the crowd thinned out a little, Uncle George's mother, Rita, came over to their side. She wrapped Aunt Clara in a hug. They stood like that for a long time, not saying anything. Then Rita gave Aunt Clara a soft pat on her cheek before returning to her family.

Maddy was amazed by the number of people who came. Many of them had memories to share. A lot of them were unfamiliar to her. Colleagues from the university, former students, friends from growing up. And then people none of them knew who Uncle George had touched in some way. A homeless man he took out for coffee occasionally, a woman who cleaned his office, the owner of a used bookstore George frequented. Maddy was impacted by each and every tale, holding on to them like puzzle pieces. If she could collect all the stories of his life, maybe she could hold on to her uncle a little longer.

The next day was Uncle George's funeral. And after that, Maddy and her mother would head home. Maddy was finishing her senior year of high school and couldn't afford to spend much more time out of the classroom. She had finals coming up and then preparations for college. Except … she wasn't sure college was the right choice anymore.

Later that evening, Maddy heard a knock on her door. "Come in."

"I want to give you something." Her aunt stood in the doorway, a folded piece of paper in her hand.

"I wanted to talk to you, too." Maddy debated how to best approach this subject with her aunt, but she decided to cut to the chase. "I'm thinking about deferring enrollment in the fall."

"What? Why?" Aunt Clara's face twisted in bewilderment.

"What do you mean, why? How can I just leave you here by yourself?" After watching Aunt Clara go through the pain of planning her own husband's funeral, Maddy didn't have the heart to walk away from her aunt and leave her on her own.

"You want to stay home from college to help me?"

"I don't want you to have to face a year all alone without Uncle George here."

"That's very sweet of you, Madeleine, but you can't. I won't let you." Aunt Clara's voice was firm.

"Why not?" This was the most practical solution. "It won't be forever, just for a year or so."

"I'm going to be very lonely without George here, but I'm not alone."

"You mean because you have God?" There was more than a hint of skepticism in her voice. Maddy wasn't quite clear on how

God worked, but people were always talking about Him like He was in the room with them or living inside of them, somehow.

"Yes, I have God, and I also have the church. They'll be here for me because they love me. Just like you."

Aunt Clara patted Maddy on the knee. "Here, this is for you. He wrote it for you once he knew ..." She choked on the words before she could finish her sentence. "Here." She handed over the piece of paper. "I'll give you some privacy." Maddy unfolded the letter and immediately recognized Uncle George's cramped handwriting.

Dear Maddy,

I want you to know I've always loved you like you were my own daughter, and I'm as proud as if you were. I wish so badly I could be there to watch you go to college and become a professional artist like you've always wanted. We've known from the beginning how talented you are. I'm so glad the world will get to see it, too.

Maddy, I know your dad would be incredibly proud of you right now. I hope someday he gets to see what an amazing woman you've become. I know without a doubt he loves you just as much as he ever did.

If you don't remember anything else I've said, remember this. As much as your family loves you, God loves you more. He is the best father. He has given you everything—freedom, love, purpose. All you have to do is follow Him. I hope I've shown you a little of the joy that God can give. I pray my life has been an example of what God can do.

Maddy, I wish you every happiness and every good thing in life, but I know hard times will come, too. They've already come for you. Hold on to God and

hold on to your family. And hold on to the incredible gift you've been given. Show the world your beautiful soul through your art.

I love you more than I can say. Love,

Uncle George

Maddy forced down the lump in her throat. She'd cried so much this week, she hadn't thought there would be any tears left to shed.

If Uncle George really believed her art was that special, maybe she owed it to him, to everyone who had supported her over the years, to give it a try. She would go to art school, and she would be the very best artist she could be. For Uncle George.

14

*B*y Wednesday afternoon, Madeleine had finished outlining the mural. The next step was underpainting, or covering the wall with large spots of color in the background she would later go over again with more detail in the foreground. But before she got too far into the painting, Madeleine needed to meet with Sam to get his approval.

She cleaned up her workspace as best as possible, straightening the drop cloth and setting aside the ladder. She took a minute to admire her work and check for any flaws. Nope, still great. She marched herself over to Sam's office and knocked on his door.

"Come in."

"Hey, Sam." Madeleine pushed open the door, trying to maintain her confident attitude. "Are you ready to see what I have so far?"

"I certainly am." Sam stood from whatever he was working on. Something that involved lots of books and coffee and legal pads. "Lead the way."

Madeleine chewed her lip while Sam surveyed her work. He sure was taking his sweet time. He stood several feet from the wall and scanned the whole drawing, making approving-sounding grunts. Then, he examined each part in detail, left-to-right. Finally, he stepped back and nodded.

"Well? What do you think?" Madeleine couldn't take the suspense anymore.

"I like it." Sam turned to her and smiled. Madeleine beamed in return. Woohoo!

"So can I start painting?" Madeleine was itching to get painting again.

"No."

What in the world?

"Why not?" Her shoulders tensed as she prepared for criticism.

"You should wait until tomorrow. The church meets tonight, and I don't want anyone accidentally touching your wet paint. In fact, you should probably clean everything up off the floor." Sam patted Madeleine on the shoulder. "Great work. I'm really looking forward to seeing the finished product."

Madeleine let out her breath. Relieved Sam didn't have another problem with the mural, Madeleine gladly rolled the drop cloth and carted all of her painting accoutrements to the creepy supply closet.

On her way out the door, Madeleine's phone rang. Seeing the caller ID, she quickly declined the call. A few minutes later, the phone rang again. Pulling it out of her pocket, Madeleine froze when she saw the number. A.J. Her fingers fumbled to accept the call.

"He-hello?" Madeleine cleared her throat. Cool, calm, and detached, she reminded herself.

"Madeleine? It's A.J." His voice came out sounding even cuter over the phone than in person, if that were possible. Madeleine's heart leapt in rebellion.

"Hey, A.J." She hadn't forgotten she was supposed to be

angry at him—or at least keeping things platonic. But talking to A.J. on the phone was so ... personal ... so intimate.

"Hey. Listen. I've been thinking a lot, and I wanted to apologize for what I said to you. I didn't mean to upset you, and I ruined a perfectly good shave ice. Would you let me make it up to you?"

"I don't know." Madeleine took a breath and tried to keep her voice neutral. "What did you have in mind?"

"Well, the teens really wanted you to come to our singing tonight."

"Just the teens?" Madeleine winced as the words came out. Would someone who was detached care how much A.J. wanted her there?

"I'd like you to come, too. Of course." A.J. said it like Madeleine should already know. Of course, he wanted her to come. "And I thought maybe we could go get coffee. Or whatever you want."

"Um, yeah. Yes. I would like that." She twirled her hair around her fingers absentmindedly but quickly stuffed her hand in her pocket when she realized what she was doing.

"Great. I'll see you at seven in the youth room."

"Okay, see you then." Madeleine walked to the parking lot in a daze.

As she ended the call, two questions loomed in her mind. Is this supposed to be a date? And do I want it to be a date?

After a dozen wardrobe changes, Madeleine finally settled on an outfit—her nicest pair of jeans and an embroidered black top with a scoop neck. And she curled her hair. And she put on a little dab of perfume.

Not that she should care, since A.J. had seen her in grungy workout clothes and drenched in river water. But, still. More and more, Madeleine found herself wanting to make a good impression on A.J. Their first meeting had been pretty terrible, but maybe future encounters would be better. Even if they would only ever be friends.

"You look nice. I take it you're coming with me to church tonight?" Aunt Clara still wasn't completely well, but she wasn't nearly as wilted and pale as the day before. She stirred something delicious on the stove.

"Yes. I thought I'd go to the singing with the teens … and A.J." Madeleine added the last part quietly and quickly, hoping Aunt Clara wouldn't make a big deal out of it.

"Oh? I take it you two have made up?" She raised an eyebrow. Madeleine had filled her in on the details of their argument the day before.

"Sort of. He wants to go out for coffee afterwards to apologize." Madeleine avoided eye contact by setting the table with plates and silverware.

"Couldn't he just say sorry over the phone or at the singing?" Clearly, Aunt Clara was prodding Madeleine to admit that something was going on between them. But the truth was, Madeleine didn't know where she stood with A.J. anymore. She hoped tonight would serve to clear things up.

"He could. He did say sorry on the phone. It was his idea. Besides, I wasn't going to turn down free food." Madeleine continued trying to downplay the situation, although she caught a pleased smile on Aunt Clara's face. She grabbed two tall glasses and filled them with ice and tea from the teapot on the counter.

Aunt Clara ladled steamy pink sauce from the stove onto a waiting platter of linguine noodles. Then she sprinkled grated Parmesan cheese and stuck a sprig of parsley on top. "Voila!"

Madeleine nodded in approval. "Looks delicious."

Aunt Clara carried the platter to the kitchen table. "Sounds like A.J. is ignoring Nancy's advice."

"I think it's best to assume A.J. doesn't want to date me until he actually asks me out. I don't know yet if he ignored Nancy's advice or not." Madeleine set a bowl of bread on the table and began ladling pasta out for each of them.

"I'm pretty sure he already asked you out. You're certainly dressed like you're going on a date tonight." Aunt Clara wiggled her eyebrows.

"There's no harm in dressing nice ... just in case." Madeleine tried to give her aunt a stern, silencing glare but couldn't manage to stop smiling. Perhaps it was time she admitted what she really wanted, to be going on a date with A.J. Young.

She bowed her head as Aunt Clara led a prayer over their food. "Father, thank You for this food and for our good health. I ask for

special guidance for A.J. and Madeleine. Please lead them down the paths You'd like them to take. May this friendship please be a blessing to them both. It's in your Son's name we pray. Amen."

Madeleine was always inexplicably calmer after Aunt Clara prayed over her. Well, maybe not inexplicably. Maybe the explanation was that Aunt Clara had been right about God all along.

* * *

That night, the youth room quietly buzzed with the sound of teens chatting. As Madeleine approached the door, she realized the boy a few feet ahead of her was Mitchell. She was prepared to give a tight-lipped smile and maybe a slight nod, but Mitchell caught her off guard. He turned to hold open the door and grinned as he met her eyes.

"Hey, Madeleine. How's it going?"

"Um, hi. Good. Thanks. How are you?" Madeleine returned his smile as she stumbled through her words.

"Good. See ya." Mitchell gave a small wave before he headed across the room to his friends.

Madeleine spotted A.J. in the middle of a cluster of guys. She couldn't quite catch his eye, so she walked over to Sophie and Caitlin.

"You came!" Caitlin gave her a big hug.

"Yeah." Madeleine laughed. "I just had to hear A.J.'s singing voice."

"I think you might remember a couple of the songs from when you were a kid. If you sit by us, our loud voices will drown you out." Sophie smiled sweetly at her. Madeleine had a hard time imagining anything about Sophie being loud.

The girls found seats in a ring of chairs in the middle of the room. As Madeleine sat, she caught A.J. staring at her. When he grinned, she could tell all of her hard work to get ready tonight had paid off.

Slowly, the rest of the teens broke off from their groups and joined them in the circle. They each took a songbook from a stack that A.J. passed around. Madeleine flipped through, noting a lot of songs familiar to her, but also many new ones.

A.J. started off by selecting one she'd sung many times as a child. Madeleine joined in quietly at first and then a little louder as memories of Bible class and VBS came rushing back to her. Singing together with friends was something she hadn't experienced in a long time. She hadn't even realized she missed it.

Madeleine was shocked to hear a beautiful, strong soprano voice come out of Sophie and a softer, alto voice come from Caitlin. Above the singing of Sophie and Caitlin, the most gorgeous baritone rang out.

A.J. The girls weren't kidding. His voice was definitely swoon-worthy. After the first song, the teens started requesting different ones.

Madeleine sat quietly, enjoying the sound of voices mingling together, harmonizing beautifully. She read along in the songbook as she listened. After the seventh or eighth tune, A.J. pulled out his Bible.

"Turn with me to Colossians 3:11-17. Could someone read when they get there?"

Madeleine mentally slapped herself in the forehead. She'd completely forgotten to bring a Bible. Sophie wordlessly slid hers closer to Madeleine to share.

Thank you, God, for Sophie. The spontaneous nature of the prayer surprised Madeleine. She hadn't realized she felt close enough to God to do something like that. Was it the fact that she'd been immersed in the Bible and the stories of Jesus? Or was it because of time spent with Clara and A.J. and Sam?

Turner read the verses. "Here there is not Greek and Jew, circumcised and uncircumcised, barbarian, Scythian, slave, free; but Christ is all, and in all. Put on then, as God's chosen ones, holy and beloved, compassionate hearts, kindness, humility, meekness, and patience, bearing with one another and, if one has a complaint against another, forgiving each other; as the Lord has forgiven you, so you must also forgive. And above all these put on love, which binds everything together in perfect harmony. And let the peace of Christ rule in your hearts, to which indeed you were called in one body. And be thankful. Let the word of Christ dwell in you richly, teaching and admonishing one another in all wisdom, singing psalms and hymns and spiritual songs, with thankfulness in your hearts to God. And whatever you do, in word or deed, do everything in the name of the Lord Jesus, giving thanks to God the Father through him."

Madeleine's cheeks burned at the mention of forgiveness. Did A.J. choose this passage just for her tonight? She tried to make eye contact, but he continued through his lesson, not looking at her.

"The world wants you to put on all kinds of things. Put on the coolest clothes. Put the cutest picture on the internet. Put yourself in the nicest car. But as much as those things seem really great right now, ultimately, they don't matter.

"Here, Paul says to put on compassionate hearts, kindness, humility, meekness, patience, forgiveness, and—above all these —love. Those are the things that matter.

"When we sing together, we don't always have perfect harmony. I know I don't, for sure. But love binds us together in perfect harmony. Even when we disagree. Even when we make mistakes. Through everything that happens between us, love is what will smooth over everything and overpower those bad feelings."

Madeleine's self-consciousness faded away as she listened to A.J. talk. She'd never heard him teach before, and she was even more impressed by his lesson than she had been by his singing voice. No wonder he was a teacher. A.J. had a real gift for speaking.

"It's easier at some times than others to remember we are working for God. But even as you're hanging out with your friends at the pool— and especially when you're working a really terrible summer job." The older kids laughed knowingly at that. "You're to go into the world and show others God's love. The love we share with each other here when we encourage each other through singing or through kind words or through time spent together. We take that love and we share it with the world."

After A.J. finished his lesson, the teens sang a couple more songs. All night, Madeleine had been content to sit and listen, but one in particular caught her eye. The words had always resonated with her as a little girl. She'd loved the idea of God cradling her like a precious lamb or prizing her like a diamond. Caitlin must have noticed her wistful expression and called out, "Number 23!"

As Madeleine heard the words for the first time in over a decade, her eyes moistened. How she longed for that security again, just like when she was a child standing between her father and mother at church. She desperately wanted to return to those days when she was cherished by her father and had no doubts in her mind about a loving God who gave everything to be with her.

Madeleine quickly dabbed at her eyes with her thumbs. A.J. led one last song, and all the teens joined in without even glancing at their books. Joshua led everyone in a prayer. Afterwards, Madeleine surreptitiously snuck a mirror from her purse to check for mascara smudges on her face.

Satisfied, Madeleine snapped her mirror shut as Sophie and Caitlin said their goodbyes and left to find their parents. A.J. was talking to Phoebe and Jessica, so she waited until they were wrapping up their conversation.

"Hey, guys." Madeleine gave a tiny, awkward wave.

"Hey, Madeleine. Nice to see you." Phoebe smiled kindly.

"You, too." Madeleine struggled with what to say to the girls. All she really wanted was to talk to A.J. Thankfully, Jessica caught on.

"Well, we'd better be going. See you around." Jessica waved and pulled Phoebe's elbow.

"Oh, okay, well, bye then." Phoebe, confused, followed Jessica out of the room.

"Hi, there." A.J.'s soft smile melted her heart. She wanted so badly to erase all romantic feelings for him, but she couldn't. No matter how hard she tried.

"Hi." She put her hands in her pocket and took them out again. "Wanna go grab a coffee?" The tension between them seemed to have doubled since the last time they spoke. But now, instead of cold anger, there was something else ... something that made them both suddenly shy around each other.

"Sure. I love coffee." Even in the summertime, Madeleine relished the feeling of a warm cup in her hand and the taste of a nicely roasted brew. And she could use a little fortification right now.

"Oh, good." A.J. smiled, looking relieved and pleased with himself. "You love it, too?" Maybe liking coffee was some kind of prerequisite she had to meet before getting closer to A.J.

"Well … no, actually." A.J. rubbed the back of his neck and gave her a sheepish grimace.

"Really?"

"Yeah, I hate the stuff." He winced. "Then why did you ask me to coffee?"

"It seemed like the kind of thing you might like. I was just glad I guessed right."

Madeleine rolled her eyes as she laughed at him and felt the tension roll away. What a ridiculous man. His silliness and sweet desire to guess what would make her happy softened her heart even more.

"Would you rather get a milkshake?"

"Yes!" A.J. paused, his eyes hopeful and questioning. "If that's okay with you."

"A shake would be wonderful."

a round the block from the church building was an old-fashioned diner with milkshakes and ice cream sundaes, Mike's Diner. The place had remained essentially unchanged for the last twenty years, and Madeleine had many fond memories of visiting with her parents after church on a Sunday night or for a special treat after school. Madeleine ordered a strawberry cheesecake shake. A.J. ordered triple chocolate and insisted on paying. They sat in a booth, away from the three other customers there that evening.

"So, you wanted to talk?" Madeleine grimaced. She hated how her voice sounded, demanding and unforgiving, but she wanted to get explanations out of the way so they could return to being friends.

"Yes. Listen, I know I offended you by calling you sensitive. I never meant to hurt your feelings."

Good. Now Madeleine could forgive him and move on. She straightened and took a sip of her milkshake.

"But …"

But what? What more needed to be said? Her shoulders tensed.

"I think it's really important to be honest in relationships." He looked down at his hands spread out on the table. "I want to be friends with you, but it's going to be hard to do that if I'm constantly walking on eggshells."

Madeleine pressed her fingers to her temples. This was a little more complicated than she'd expected. A.J. was not willing to simply say sorry and move on.

But perhaps he was right. She wanted to have an honest relationship with A.J. Maybe the best place to start was at the beginning. She took a deep breath.

"Has my Aunt Clara told you about my history with this church?

Why we left?"

"A little." A.J. nodded. "I'd like to hear what you have to say about it."

"I was ten when my father left us. It destroyed my mother, but we kept coming to church—here in Shady Springs." She picked up the straw wrapper lying on the table, folding it into a tiny square. "My mother clung to her belief and the church as her one comfort. Until one of the ladies at church here, Nancy Jones, told my mother it was her fault my father left." Her voice took on a tone of bitterness, but she couldn't help it. "She said if my mom had been a better wife, then Dad wouldn't have run off like he did." She paused, then met A.J.'s gaze. "And I heard the whole thing."

"I'm sorry. That must have been really difficult." A.J. started to reach his hand out, as if to comfort, but stopped.

"It was. It made me so angry, and it devastated my mother." Madeleine's brow creased as she remembered the pain and humiliation her mother had gone through. "After that, Mom stopped coming to church and stopped bringing me, too. A few months later, she got a job offer in Kansas City, and we left."

Madeleine realized the straw wrapper in her hands was torn to shreds. She piled up the million tiny pieces in a heap on the table.

"We visited churches here and there in Kansas City, but the damage had already been done. Mom doesn't trust Christians anymore, and neither do I. No offense, but so many of them are hypocrites. Saying one thing and meaning something else. Like, saying Jesus was all about loving people and God is love, but then treating other people terribly."

She took a breath and ranted on. "I mean, when I wait tables back in Kansas City, the very worst time to work is always when the church crowd comes in on Sunday afternoon."

"I'm sorry to hear that." A.J. winced in sympathy. "You know we're not all like Nancy Jones. And honestly, I'm surprised she said something like that." His brow wrinkled in concern. "Was there anyone else who treated you badly, or was it just her?"

Madeleine's gaze drifted to the corner of the ceiling as she thought. "I don't know for sure. I don't think anyone came out and said anything, but it wasn't only Nancy who hurt us. All of our friends stopped hanging out with us. It was like once my parents were separated, no one knew what to do with us. We didn't fit the mold anymore." She sighed. "All I know for sure is that it was enough for my mom to want to leave. My guess is that it was a lot of little things, you know? I'm still not sure coming here was a good idea." She glanced down at the table and stirred her milkshake.

"So why did you come here?" he asked.

She shrugged. "Aunt Clara. Through everything with the divorce, she was there for us. As hard as I tried to say no to this job, I just couldn't."

"Well, I'm glad you came even if you aren't."

She returned his soft smile. "Thanks. I guess I told you all that to say that being thoughtful is important to me. It was a lack of tact that caused Nancy to say what she did. Being sensitive doesn't have to be bad."

"You're right, it doesn't." A.J. paused to take a sip of his milkshake, and she could picture wheels in his head spinning. "I don't want you to harden your heart against all Christians just because you've been hurt before."

Madeleine had never thought of her heart as hard, but maybe that's what had happened. After so many years of trying to protect herself by putting up emotional armor, maybe she'd been too closed off. She was crushed to think that A.J. might see her as hard-hearted.

"I'm sorry if I've come off as rude," she said quietly.

"No, Madeleine." He waved his hands. "No, I didn't mean that. I think you are really nice. I like you a lot."

"Thanks." She couldn't keep the grin off her face. "I like you a lot, too." As if it wasn't blatantly obvious.

"Thanks." A.J. returned her smile, and her stomach flipped. "I'm impressed with how quickly you got to know the youth group. And how much you care about your aunt."

A.J. placed his fingers over Madeleine's on the table. Her heart skipped a beat. He'd made a simple gesture, but they were a giant step from where they stood a moment before. Madeleine had to force her gaze up and away from A.J.'s hand and into his eyes.

"I don't want you to throw away a relationship with God because of one mistake someone else made." His thumb stroked the back of her hand before drawing away.

Madeleine shook her head, trying to focus on the conversation. "Actually … can you keep a secret from Aunt Clara?"

"I think so. What is it?" A.J.'s eyebrows knitted in concern.

"I've been enjoying reading the Bible." She ducked her head a little.

A.J. gave a burst of laughter. "I'm glad to hear you're liking the Bible. Why am I not allowed to tell Clara?"

"Because I'm afraid of disappointing her. I'm afraid if she knows I'm having questions about God, she'll assume I'm ready to get baptized tonight. And I don't want to hurt her."

He nodded. "I won't tell her if you promise to come to me or Sam with questions. You need to talk to her eventually, but I won't talk to her before you do."

"All right, I promise to go to someone with my questions." She gave a small smile.

"Any in particular you're having right now?" He leaned forward slightly.

"No ... well, maybe." Where to begin?

"Go ahead." A.J. smiled encouragingly as Madeleine tried to form her shapeless thoughts into words.

"Do you really believe all of it? I mean, do you believe that Jesus was God and that all the things in the Bible are true?"

"I do. I really believe it." His eyes were clear and without any doubts. "Then why ... why do Christians act the way they do when they're supposed to be like Jesus?" Madeleine went on, unable to stop the questions spilling out. "I mean, if God has truly transformed them, why are they still sinful? Why do they act like the rest of the world?"

"That's a good question, and I understand why you're asking it, especially considering everything you told me." A.J. paused thoughtfully while taking another sip of his shake. Madeleine looked down at hers, almost all there and melting by the minute.

"People make mistakes." A.J. shook his head a little. "Even when they are supposed to be listening to the voice of the Holy Spirit, they still mess up. The real difference between Christians and the rest of the world is that we've asked for God's forgiveness. The Bible says we are continuously undergoing sanctification, like God is scrubbing us clean and making us more like Him, but we still have the freedom to make the choices we want. And sometimes we choose wrong."

Madeleine nodded. "I'm just still having a hard time reconciling the Jesus I read about in the Bible and the Christians I see every day. I mean, you are great and Sam and Aunt Clara, but not everyone is."

"I'm not perfect. You've seen that already, so I know you're not surprised." A.J. paused, his brow furrowed in thought. "I want you to become a Christian, I really do. I think you will be blown away by what a relationship with God is like. But I don't want you going into it thinking everything will be easy and perfect. God's people are still people. Someone will hurt your feelings and make a mistake. But with God's help, you can forgive them and love them. And they can forgive you and love you, too."

"Thanks, A.J.," Madeleine said, "for answering my questions, and for the milkshake. I really hated being mad at you."

"Me, too." His gaze met hers for a moment, and her heart filled. Even if she could never be with A.J. in the way she wanted, even if nothing ever came of her attraction to him, she would be grateful to have his friendship. He really was an incredible guy.

"What about counseling? Have you ever thought of being a counselor?" He'd certainly shown an aptitude for listening.

"I was an excellent camp counselor for two summers."

"That's not the type I meant." She threw a piece of straw wrapper at him. It floated down to the table harmlessly.

"I don't know." He wrinkled his nose. "That seems to involve lots of time sitting down and lots of grad school." He shook his finger at her. "Keep trying, Madeleine."

Madeleine took a big sip of her strawberry shake and smiled. Despite all the questions floating around her mind, she was truly happy tonight. Maybe her joy came from the delicious ice cream. Maybe, but probably not.

* * *

A.J. sighed deeply as he closed the door to his modest home, which wasn't far from the center of Shady Springs. Nothing was, really. But the property was still much too isolated for his liking.

Compared to living in the city, his two acres made him feel like a farmer or a cowboy or something. Two whole acres was too much for just one man, too much for him, at least. He usually hated living alone, but right now he was grateful to have some peace and quiet to process what had happened tonight.

A.J. had wanted to stay at the diner and talk through the night with Madeleine, but he knew if he didn't limit his time with her, something bad and irreversible might happen. Not that falling in love with Madeleine Mullins would be bad. Wait. Yes, it would. He gave himself a mental shake. It would be very bad.

Fall in love was a little strong. He wasn't quite there yet. He barely knew her. But he couldn't deny that was where things were headed. He'd only met the girl about a week ago, but it seemed like much longer. Especially since they'd just had their second date. Kind of.

Obviously, she was very attractive. No one could deny that. The way her long hair was sort-of-brown and sort-of-blonde and always hung in curls. The way her brown eyes had little flecks of gold and green that sparkled when she laughed. The way her full lips curled into a smile so easily.

A.J. took a deep breath. Maybe if he ignored them, his feelings for Madeleine would go away. Like she would go away at the end of the summer. Madeleine was only here for a little while and then gone. But, of course, the main reason he couldn't get involved with her was because, deep down inside, she didn't have the same values and priorities. He knew he could never marry someone who wasn't a Christian. And dating was only a means to an end. If he wanted to marry a Christian woman, then he needed to date a Christian woman.

The problem with a small town like Shady Springs was, there weren't a whole lot of single women, Christian or otherwise. His family would be quick to remind him that he'd had plenty of chances to find single women at their home church in Little Rock. Or at his Christian university alma mater. But those chances were gone, and the older he got, the more weddings he attended, and the more women his age were happily married. He'd even received a birth announcement last week from his college roommate, which put him even further behind where his friends were.

It's not a race. A.J. heard a voice in the innermost parts of his conscience. He was reminded of one of his favorite Bible verses, Matthew 6:33. But seek first the kingdom of God and his righteousness, and all these things will be added to you. A.J. knew life didn't begin with marriage. He already had a full life that he loved. There were more important things than finding a wife. And there were plenty of examples of single people in the Bible, Jesus and Paul chief among them. He just hoped he could settle down with someone. Someday.

Ping!

A.J. pulled his cell phone out of his pocket and saw he had a text message.

Madeleine: Thx for the milkshake and for answering my questions.

Have a great night!

A.J. quickly opened his messaging app, but then stumbled over what to say in reply. What words would encourage Madeleine's friendship but not romantic affections? What would keep her close but not too close?

A.J.: Anytime. Good night!

Sweet and simple. If only his emotions could be tied into a

neat knot as easily as that. He sat on the small couch in his living room and flipped on the news, hoping to distract himself from his own problems. But every commercial was for engagement rings. Or for a grocery store with an actress who resembled Madeleine. Or a pet store with a cocker spaniel that reminded A.J. of Madeleine's curly hair. Okay, time to turn off the TV.

A.J. finally turned to the place he should have started all along, prayer. Time spent with God at the end of a long day was exactly what his mind and heart needed. Throughout all of his life, the only surefire thing to get his anxious and active body to truly be still was prayer. A.J. scooted back on the sofa and rested his head in his hands.

Father God, I know You have a plan for me and a will for my life. I pray You would guide me. I have no idea what I'm doing with Madeleine. I have such a strong connection with her. And I can tell she is a good person. Please soften her heart for You, God. Please keep me from getting in over my head.

* * *

A.J.: I'm headed over to clean the building. Don't panic and attack me or anything.

Madeleine: Why in the world would I do a crazy thing like that???

A.J.: I don't know … ;)

Madeleine smiled to herself as she stuck her phone in her bag. She'd gotten an early start and was pleased with the progress she'd made so far. In several plastic tubs, Madeleine had bright greens and oranges and light browns and pinks. The colors she'd mixed would flash vibrantly against the plain white of the primer in contrast with the rest of the gray walls. Maybe the church would like this mural so much they'd ask her to help paint the rest of the building.

Wait, no. She didn't want to stay and paint the rest of the

building. She wanted to get home. As soon as possible. Right. Something about this town lulled her into complacency. Shady Springs was just so ... peaceful. That was the only way Madeleine could think to describe it.

Every time she came back to visit, Madeleine was reminded of how much she loved this small town with its tree-filled Spring Park, its antique shops, and old favorite restaurants like Mike's Diner. She loved how everyone waved at each other and how people still honked to say hello.

But she couldn't stay. Madeleine had a life in Kansas City and a career to think about. No way could she make a living painting murals for small town churches. Besides, hanging over all of Shady Springs like a black cloud was the threat of running into Nancy. Madeleine hadn't seen her since the ice cream social, but the time was coming when she would have to face the past. She just wasn't sure if she would ever be ready.

Madeleine turned to the can of black paint and dipped her small roller brush in, coating it. With broad strokes, Madeleine began creating the shadow of a cross in the middle of the wall. She would start here, with darkness, and move out. Soon, the wall would be covered with the bright green of grass and trees, the deep blues of sky and water, bold pink and purple sunsets, and rich brown flesh in every shade. Faces would feature prominently in Madeleine's mural. The men and women who Jesus touched and healed and changed. The more Madeleine got into Matthew, the more she saw that the story of Jesus was the story of people. Jesus loved people, and Madeleine wanted to show that in her mural.

Even though Madeleine had been warned, she was still surprised when A.J. showed up, and she almost dropped a brush full of paint on the floor. As it was, she caught the business end of the brush with her hands and ended up a complete mess. Thank goodness the clothes she wore were already covered in splatters. A little more paint wouldn't hurt them.

"Hey. Did I scare you?" A.J.'s ever-present good humor shone through in his voice.

"Only a little." Madeleine wiped her hands on a cloth.

"At least you didn't get paint all over yourself." A.J. gave a sarcastic laugh.

"Yeah. That would be a disaster. I have a fancy dinner to go to later, and I don't want my ball gown ruined." Madeleine twirled in her grungy overall shorts and tennis shoes.

"What? So do I! We must have been invited to the same fancy dinner!" A.J. gestured to his holey jeans and faded T-shirt.

"Perhaps we should go together." Madeleine curtsied, pulling the hem of her shorts.

"Enchanté, mademoiselle." A.J. bowed. "May I have this dance?"

Madeleine took A.J.'s outstretched hands and waltzed around the hallway in his arms, twirling faster and faster until they both collapsed in a laughing heap, out of breath.

"How about we both get back to work, and I'll swing by when I'm done cleaning?" A.J. stood and pulled Madeleine up with him.

"Sounds good to me." Although she had stopped dancing, Madeleine's head still spun. For a moment, she allowed herself to relish the memory of A.J.'s hands around hers and the clean smell of his T- shirt, then she brushed off her overalls. "Back to work."

Madeleine took a few deep breaths, clearing her thoughts. Was it her imagination, or was A.J. very flirtatious today? The dancing was pure silliness and fun, but did it mean something more to him? Maybe A.J. acted like that with all of his friends, but Madeleine sure didn't. Not with anyone as handsome as A.J., at least. Not with anyone who smelled that nice.

Focus, Madeleine. Expelling one more huge breath, Madeleine picked up her brush again and got busy.

Soon, she'd found a good rhythm, covering the wall in a

veritable rainbow of color, radiating out from the shadow of the cross. By the time A.J. returned a few hours later, bright paint coated half of the wall's surface.

A.J. walked toward her with two paper cups in one hand and a 2 liter of soda in the other, his jeans splattered in soapy water. A light sheen of sweat covered his forehead. He plopped down on the floor and patted the carpet next to him, indicating Madeleine should join him.

"Ready for a break?" A.J. set down the cups and opened the soda bottle. No sizzle of fizz or burst of bubbles accompanied the opening, just quiet. "Hmm." A.J. held the bottle up to his face, inspecting the expiration date. "I'm not sure how long this has been sitting in the fridge. Wanna try it?"

"Um, no. Not really. I'd be shocked if that thing cost more than a dollar even before it expired. Definitely not worth the risk."

A.J. poured her a cup anyway, and Madeleine eyed it cautiously.

"Not terrible." A.J. gulped down his soda and poured himself another helping.

"Blech. Yes, it is terrible. It's completely flat." Madeleine made a face and set her cup down, then scooted it as far away as possible. "Why are you still drinking that ... that swill?"

"Swill?" He raised one eyebrow. "I have never heard an actual person use that word before."

"You know, I don't think I have either, but it fits the situation perfectly."

"Maybe. But I happen to like swill." He downed another mouthful for emphasis.

"That's disgusting. I can't watch." She turned away in mock horror. "Don't watch, then." A.J. gestured to the mural. "Tell me about this. I know you're a famous artist, but this just looks like a bunch of blobs."

"I'm almost finished with the underpainting. I'm going to

add more detail next. See, there are four quadrants, and each of those will have a vignette of Jesus performing a miracle or teaching people. And in the middle—"

"Jesus on the cross. I like it." He leaned back and nodded.

"Yeah. I haven't decided yet how I want to paint Jesus on the cross. Nothing too graphic, since it's for the kids. I've certainly studied my fair share of crucifixions in art history. They can vary in how ... realistic they are."

"I kind of like it as a shadow. I think ... the point is not how Jesus looked. What matters is what Jesus did for us."

"That's exactly what Sam said." Madeleine reexamined the shadowed cross. "You may be right. I could add just enough highlights to show what it is but leave the rest in shadow. Then show light radiating out behind it with some white there and there." Madeleine pointed to the wall as she talked, getting more animated as she saw the finished picture in her head. "You could be an artist, you know. Do you think that's your calling?"

"Oh, no, definitely not. I'll leave that to the professionals, Madeleine Mullins." A.J. stood and took the cups and half empty soda bottle with him. "I bid you good day, madam. It has been a pleasure." A.J. tipped an imaginary hat and bowed low.

"The pleasure was all mine, good sir. But please take your swill with you." Madeleine stood and curtsied, then watched A.J. walk away.

* * *

That evening, once Madeleine got to a good stopping point and stored her supplies, she walked over to Sam's office. She'd promised A.J. she would talk to someone if she had any questions. Madeleine could see Sam's car in the parking lot from the windows in the hall, so she knew he was around. She figured Sam could be trusted not to report everything she asked back to Aunt Clara.

Madeleine stood at the door for a minute. Nerves fizzed inside of her. Her hand hovered over the door, poised to knock. Finally, she gave a brief tap.

"Yes?" Sam called from inside.

"Do you have a minute to talk?" Madeleine poked her head into Sam's office.

"Of course, I do. Come in, come in." Sam rose from his seat and waved her inside. He cleared a stack of books from a chair in front of his desk and dusted it off before offering the chair to Madeleine.

"Thanks." She sat gingerly, trying not to add any paint stains to the already grimy wood.

"How's the mural going?" Sam sat behind his desk and swiveled toward Madeleine.

"It's coming along nicely. Everything's still a little fuzzy right now. It doesn't look like much, but once I start adding the detail, it'll all come into focus."

"That's good." Sam smiled kindly. He paused a beat and then asked, "So, what can I do for you?"

Madeleine wondered if he sensed she had come to talk about more than just the mural, but she wasn't sure where to begin. She picked at a spot of yellow paint she hadn't quite washed off of her hand. "Sam, why do you believe in Jesus?"

Sam sighed. "Well, I can tell you why I believe, but I think the answer is different for everyone. I'll start with the facts." He began to tick off on his fingers. "First, we know from historical accounts that Jesus was a real person. Second, we know Jesus Himself claimed to be the Son of God. And third, we know the apostles died defending the claim that Jesus was the Messiah."

"So, you believe the Bible is true?" Madeleine shifted in her seat. "You don't think someone came along later and changed things to say that Jesus was the Son of God?"

"I really believe it." Sam nodded. "Beyond the facts of the

Bible, I've seen the way God works in the lives of the people who follow Him."

Madeleine shook her head. "I haven't. Not really. It seems to me Christians are as bad as the rest of the world."

Sam's mouth turned down, and his eyes grew sad. "It can be that way, sometimes. But those people are not allowing God to truly change them."

Maybe. Madeleine still wasn't convinced. She'd seen too many so- called Christians who acted nothing like Jesus.

"I know God changed me," Sam went on. "And he gave my family— my foster family at the children's home—the strength and patience to raise some very difficult young men." Sam chuckled. "I was not easy to live with sometimes, but they loved me through the hard times and encouraged me—well, pushed me, really—to go to college. I wouldn't be here today if it wasn't for people who loved God. And I don't mean here in Shady Springs. I mean, I wouldn't be alive."

"Wow." Madeleine took a breath as the magnitude of that thought sunk in.

"You know," Sam said. "I'm always surprised more artists aren't Christians."

"What do you mean?" Madeleine cocked her head a bit.

"I mean, how do we even know what's great art and what's just junk?" Sam leaned toward Madeleine with a twinkle in his eye.

"Well, we have formulas for that. Like the golden ratio or the rule of thirds." These were concepts Madeleine had learned about in some of her early art lessons in junior high.

Sam gestured to his office window and the trees outside. "And aren't those all found in nature? Weren't they created by God?"

"Perhaps." Madeleine frowned. "But what if it's just evolution?"

"Ah." He pointed his finger at her. "Why would we need to evolve our sense of aesthetics? What purpose would that serve?"

Madeleine found herself getting caught up in Sam's enthusiasm. The man seemed to really enjoy a good debate. Her mention of evolution didn't throw him off or offend him, so she kept on with her line of reasoning. "Maybe it's a random side effect of some other skill we developed. Or maybe we needed it to find good mates."

"Okay." Sam stroked his chin. "So, do you always use the golden ratio in your art? Can that explain why any piece is considered to be a masterpiece?"

"Well, it's all very subjective." She shrugged. "I mean, one man's trash

is another man's treasure, right? I certainly don't have the same taste as some of my professors."

"Yes, but can't we all agree Van Gogh was a genius?" Sam got more excited as he talked. "Or Michelangelo, Raphael, Carravaggio? Have you ever been deeply moved by a work of art?"

"Of course." Why else had she become an artist except that it called to her? Maybe even on a spiritual level.

"So, what is it that causes humans to recognize beauty or genius?" Sam folded his hands on the desk.

Madeleine twisted her mouth in thought. "I don't know, but I think I know what your answer is."

"There has to be a higher power. There just has to be. Our very souls, our sense of justice, and our sense of beauty call out to Him." Sam patted his chest over his heart. "Can't you feel it, right here?"

"Sometimes I think I can." Madeleine sighed and rubbed at the yellow paint on her hands. "Doesn't it all seem impossible? A God who created the world and also lived in it? A God who can forgive everyone of everything?"

"It does sometimes, yes." Sam nodded slowly. "But that's what makes it all so wonderful."

Madeleine took a breath and stared up at the ceiling before asking her next question. "Was it difficult … to forgive all the people who hurt you? Your parents? The people from foster care?" Madeleine winced a little as she asked. She knew it was such a personal question, and she wasn't sure he would respond.

For a long while, Sam sat with the question hanging in the air. "It was hard," he said, finally. "But it was even harder to forgive myself."

Madeleine narrowed her eyes, confused. "What do you mean?"

"I mean, when I finally sorted through all my emotions, all of the anger and sadness and bitterness, I realized that I blamed myself for a lot." He rested his folded hands against his chin. "I think my biggest hurdle to overcome was my disbelief in a God who would forgive me, who would choose me. Why should God pick me when even my own parents didn't want me?"

Madeleine's eyes stung. She'd never come out and said it, but Sam's words hit on her exact fears. Her own father had packed up and left. Why should God love her?

"How did you do it? How did you overcome all of that?" Madeleine blinked quickly.

"I won't lie, it was very difficult. But when I finally realized God's love was there whether or not I accepted it …" He shook his head. "Madeleine, there is a love there—waiting for you— and it is more wonderful than you can imagine."

Madeleine sat for a minute and let Sam's words wash over her. What would it feel like to finally let everything go? Could God's love change her life like it changed Sam's?

"Thank you for sharing with me. You've given me a lot to think about." Madeleine stood slowly.

Sam rose and placed a hand on her shoulder. "I hope you

know you can come to me anytime. I don't mind discussing the difficult topics, in fact, those are my very favorite kind."

"I appreciate it, Sam." Madeleine smiled. "I'm sure I'll have many more questions. But I need a little while to sort through everything."

He patted her shoulder. "You know where to find me when you're ready to talk again."

By Thursday night, Madeleine had finished the underpainting, and by Friday evening, she'd made quite a bit of progress on the detail of the mural. This was her favorite part of the whole process, mixing the colors on the wall, watching nothing turn into something. She loved the feel of her brush as it sliced in clean lines or blurred the wet paint or flitted in light flicks of the wrist across the wall.

Before heading home to Aunt Clara's house for dinner, Madeleine went through the ritual of cleaning her brushes, making sure all of her paint was properly sealed, and storing everything in the supply closet. She hoped to talk A.J. into breakfast Saturday morning and wasn't sure what time she'd be back to work on Saturday. She didn't want to leave a huge mess in the hallway, in case someone came by.

Once home, Madeleine headed straight upstairs to shower and change into clean clothes, only pausing to say a quick hello to Aunt Clara across the hall. When she emerged from the steamy bathroom, Madeleine could smell something cheesy and savory cooking in the kitchen. And rolls, with butter. Mmm. Aunt Clara was really going all out tonight. Maybe she should rethink the sweatpants she'd laid out on her bed.

After changing into a clean T-shirt and mostly clean jeans, Madeleine walked downstairs toward the kitchen. A timer beeped, and the oven door slammed. Madeleine rounded the corner and found Aunt Clara hovering over a pot of vegetables, with a steaming casserole dish and breadbasket on the counter.

"Wow! This is a lot of food!" Madeleine racked her brain. "Are we having company? Did I forget?"

"Yes, and no. We are having company. And I did not tell you about it." Aunt Clara swiveled suddenly, distracted by a shrieking kettle on the stove, and poured the hot water into a waiting teapot. "I haven't made this much food in a long time. I'm worried I've forgotten something."

"Would you like me to set the table? How many places?" She turned to the drawer where Aunt Clara kept the placemats and cloth napkins.

"Three."

"Just three? Why did you make so much food?" Madeleine pulled out three cloth napkins.

"I was afraid there wouldn't be enough. And it's difficult to halve this casserole recipe. We'll have to eat the leftovers for a day ... or two." Aunt Clara pointed down the hall with a spoon. "I thought we could eat in the dining room. I hardly ever use it for actual eating. We should have dinner in there more often."

"So, who is it? Who's coming over?"

Aunt Clara finished stirring the green beans on the stove and looked straight at Madeleine. "Nancy Jones."

Madeleine stopped cold. Nancy was literally the last person she expected to show up for dinner tonight. Well, maybe not the very last person, but almost. What in the world was Aunt Clara thinking? And why would Nancy accept the invitation to eat a meal with Madeleine?

Before she could ask Aunt Clara any of the questions burning in her mind, the doorbell rang. Madeleine knew she should offer to get the door, but she stood stock still, reeling from the shock of what Aunt Clara had said.

"Maddy? I know you're upset. Just try to be polite and listen to what Nancy has to say. Please?" Aunt Clara left to answer the door without waiting for a confirmation.

"Welcome! Come in!"

Madeleine could hear the sounds of Nancy walking inside, talking with Aunt Clara. She busied herself with setting the table in an attempt to distract herself from her thoughts. Be polite. Do it for Aunt Clara.

When Nancy walked in, Madeleine tried to give a smile, but her lips never parted. From the expression on Aunt Clara's face, her smile did not have the intended effect and probably looked a bit more like a grimace.

Madeleine turned to the silverware drawer, pulling out three forks, three knives, and three teaspoons. She stacked the three cloth napkins on three plates, then walked into the dining room without a word as Aunt Clara talked enough for the both of them.

"Would you like tea? Or water? I think we have some lemonade, too." Madeleine took a deep breath and tried to center her thoughts. Her stomach churned. What's the worst that could happen tonight? I could get into a fistfight with Nancy. Madeleine almost laughed out loud at the thought of her wrestling with the older woman over Aunt Clara's dining room table.

"I'll just have water, thank you." Nancy sounded almost as nervous as Madeleine.

Her heart softened a little for the woman. At least they were both being forced into this by Aunt Clara. Madeleine would have more than a few words for her aunt before the night was over.

"Would you pour the drinks, Maddy?" Aunt Clara called over her shoulder as she carried the hot dishes one by one to the table.

As Madeleine pulled the glasses out of the cabinet and poured the drinks—one water for Nancy and two teas for Madeleine and her aunt—she tried to listen to the conversation in the dining room. Their muffled voices sounded pleasant. Not at all the tone of conversation Madeleine planned to have with her aunt as soon as Nancy was gone. Obviously, Nancy knew about this dinner, unlike Madeleine. They must have planned this whole thing together. Madeleine would've been furious if she had time to think about it. But she was still too shocked and too polite to start yelling at her aunt in front of company.

She brought the drinks in and sat down, avoiding Nancy's gaze, but the only spot available was across the table from her. Madeleine tried to catch her aunt's eye to give her some nonverbal chastisement, but Aunt Clara wouldn't make eye contact with her. Good. Maybe she was feeling a little guilty for springing this surprise dinner party on her. The dinner party would be the worst in history if everyone refused to look at each other.

"Let's pray." Aunt Clara grabbed Madeleine's and Nancy's hands and indicated that they should grab each other's hands.

Madeleine quickly closed her eyes and pretended she hadn't seen Aunt Clara. She risked a quick peek at Nancy's face and saw disappointment, but maybe that was just a shadow from the dim lighting.

"Father God, thank You for the opportunity to come together and eat a meal as friends and family. God, I pray our conversation tonight would reflect the love You have for us and the grace You've given us. Thank You for Nancy and for Madeleine. It's in the name of Jesus we pray these things. Amen."

"Amen," echoed Madeleine and Nancy.

Aunt Clara chatted away about her garden and the weather while she dished up heaping portions of cheesy chicken and rice casserole, fresh green beans, and steaming hot rolls. Madeleine nodded politely and helped pass plates but was not really listening to anything Aunt Clara said. After a few minutes of silent chewing, Clara finally hit on the real purpose behind their eating together.

"Madeleine, I asked Nancy here tonight because I think it's

important for both of you to face this head on. Madeleine, you've been living with anger and hurt in your heart for far too long. Ever since you were a child. Nancy, you also have hurt in your heart, and guilt. It's time you both confess what's been weighing on you."

Madeleine gaped up at her aunt mid-chew. What did Aunt Clara want her to say? To her great relief, Nancy spoke first.

"Madeleine, you need to know first and foremost that I am very sorry. For everything I said to your mother. For all of the hurt I've caused. I'm … I'm very sorry." She shook her head.

"Why did you say it? I've always wanted to ask you that. Why would you say such a hurtful thing?" Madeleine tried not to glare at Nancy, but it was very hard. Aunt Clara was right; she really did have a lot of anger in her heart toward the woman. She balled up her napkin under the table.

"Your father, he meant so much to me. Especially after … after I lost my Jason." Nancy's gaze drifted to her hands in her lap. She took a deep breath.

"Jason was her son," Aunt Clara said as she patted Nancy on the arm. "Yes. Jason died when he was only nineteen, in a car accident," Nancy continued, her eyes misty. "He and Henry, your father, were always very close as boys. Jason brought Henry to church with him and convinced him to go to church camp, and eventually, college with him. Jason was the reason Henry became a Christian." She smiled at the memory.

"I never knew that," Madeleine said softly. She shifted in her seat. "Henry always made sure to visit or write letters after Jason died. He started to become like a second son to me." Nancy's brow wrinkled. "That's why … that's why I was so shocked when I found out about everything that had been happening."

"You mean the affair? Or the alcohol?" Madeleine had a hard time speaking about her father without venom soaking her words. She tugged at the napkin in her hands.

"Both. I thought it must not be true." Nancy shook her head. "Surely, Henry wasn't capable of something like that."

"But he was." Madeleine tossed her napkin on the table.

"Yes, he was. I was wrong to blame your mother. I was just so ... It was like losing a son all over again. I wanted to do everything I could to hang onto the memory of Henry I had—the memory of a handsome, kind, talented boy—I lashed out at your mother because she was the first person I could think to blame." Nancy ducked her head, her shoulders stooped.

"Even though it wasn't her fault." Madeleine crossed her arms. She knew Nancy was trying to apologize, but she couldn't let everything go quite that easily.

"At the time, I thought it must be someone's fault." She wiped a tear with her napkin. "When I didn't blame your mother anymore, I blamed myself. It took me years to realize the only one to blame is Henry."

"Why did you let it go on so long? Why didn't you call my mother?" Madeleine sat straight. She was glad to finally have an apology, but maybe it was too little, too late.

"Oh, I did. I wrote her a letter after you two had moved to Kansas City. I reckon she wasn't ready to read it yet." Nancy shook her head. "I wouldn't be surprised if she threw it away when she saw my name on the envelope."

"Thank you for telling me." Madeleine looked down at her plate. She wasn't sure what to do with this new information. What Nancy did was inexcusable, and Madeleine was still angry about what she'd said and about everything that had happened after. But maybe the time had come to move on.

"I'm sorry I didn't tell you sooner. There's no excuse for how I behaved, but I hope knowing everything helps you understand."

"It does."

"Do you think ... do you think you could ever forgive me?"

Madeleine stared back into Nancy's pleading eyes. Could she? Could she really forgive this woman? Madeleine searched her heart. The anger and hurt had been growing inside of her for many years now, and she might need many more years to slowly unravel its tangled knots. But could she start that journey? Could she finally let go of her anger?

16

"I have one more question for you. Something's been bugging me." Madeleine fiddled with the hem of her napkin for a minute. She raised her gaze to the woman across the table. "What's that?" Nancy asked.

"Why did you tell A.J. Young to stay away from me?" She blurted it out quickly, almost embarrassed to ask.

"Is that what he said?" Nancy furrowed her eyebrows. "No, it's what I overheard." She bit her lip.

"Well, then you'll remember I didn't tell him to stay away from you. I told him to be careful. I said it to protect you, Madeleine, both of you. I knew from your aunt you hadn't returned to church. A.J. would never seriously date anyone who isn't a Christian. It would do more harm than good for him to lead you on." Nancy laid her hands out on the table. "I'm sorry if I hurt your feelings. I wasn't trying to. Quite the opposite, actually." She grimaced. "I'm still sticking my foot in my mouth at my age."

Madeleine nodded, somewhat satisfied. She absentmindedly speared a green bean and twirled her fork as she thought. Maybe she wasn't ready to become best friends with Nancy, but she was ready to let go of her anger. She'd spent ten years hating and fearing her, and it had only brought trouble. Enough was enough.

"I think I can … I think I can forgive you." A wave of relief slowly washed over Madeleine as she spoke the words.

Nancy's face broke into a glowing grin. What a weight had been lifted, and how happy she was. Forgiveness was the right choice.

"Oh, I'm so happy!" Aunt Clara clapped her hands. "You have no idea.

I'm just so glad to hear you say that. Now, who wants pie?"

Madeleine and Nancy laughed. "Maybe we should finish our dinner first, Aunt Clara."

"Yes, of course. Let me know when you're ready." She sat for only a moment before announcing, "I need to celebrate! I'm going to go get the coffee ready!" Aunt Clara leapt up and practically skipped off to the kitchen. The three women spent the rest of the evening catching up, drinking coffee, and eating Aunt Clara's delicious chocolate pie. It was velvety and rich and the exact thing to celebrate the end of a grudge and the beginning of a friendship.

"I remember when you were first born," Nancy said. "We had a big baby shower at church for you, well, as big as possible with how small we were back then. And your mother did your nursery up in pink bunny rabbits, so I made a little pink bunny lovey for you."

"Pinky Rabbit? You made Pinky Rabbit?" Madeleine had loved that little rabbit. Funny, Mom had never mentioned Nancy made it for her.

"I sure did. That and lots of baby clothes." Nancy smiled. "I was tickled to get to sew for a baby girl again."

"I never knew you made me all those things … thank you."

"You're welcome, dear. You know, you were the cutest little thing with your big mop of curly hair. But you sure gave your mom and dad lots of trouble."

"I know. That's why Aunt Clara came."

"That's right. Best decision I ever made," Aunt Clara said.

"Because then you met Uncle George." Madeleine nudged her aunt. "I sure did. Moving to Shady Springs changed my life."

"Well, you're welcome. For being such a difficult baby." Madeleine raised her eyebrows mischievously.

"Yes, thank you. You were extremely difficult, but you've gotten much better since then. Still a bit of a pain sometimes ..."

"Hey!" Madeleine hit her aunt's knee.

Nancy peered at the clock and frowned. "It's getting late. I should get home. Thank you so much for dinner, Clara. And thank you, Madeleine, for everything."

As Nancy headed toward the door, she turned to Madeleine again. "One more thing from me before I go. I want you to know I'm not angry at your father anymore. I forgave him a long time ago. Henry is just as broken and sinful as the rest of us." Nancy patted her on the arm. "I know forgiving him will be much harder than forgiving me, but think of how good it will feel to let that go."

Madeleine waved goodbye and mulled over Nancy's parting words. That wound would never heal. Her father's leaving had cut too deep. And the years of absence and hurt had infected her heart beyond the point of healing. No, a simple act of forgiveness would never cure the disease in her heart left by her father.

"Well, that went much better than I thought it would." Aunt Clara's cheerful voice instantly infuriated Madeleine. What right did she have to be pleased with herself?

"Um, excuse me. I have a few words for you." She turned on her aunt angrily.

"Oh?" Aunt Clara rested her hand on Madeleine's shoulder, but Madeleine quickly brushed it off. She wasn't in the mood for warm and fuzzy right now.

"Like, how dare you? And what in the world were you thinking? I can't believe you invited her over without asking me!" Madeleine's voice rose in pitch with each word. She hated how juvenile she sounded, but she couldn't keep the hurt from her voice.

"I knew you wouldn't agree to this if I asked. Nancy agreed to give it a try, and I had a feeling you'd be too polite to yell at her."

"How do you know I wouldn't have agreed to it?" Madeleine waved her hands in frustration.

"Because you're just like your parents." Clara gave a sigh.

"What is that supposed to mean?" How dare she bring Mom and Dad into this.

"All three of you are exactly the same, terrified of confrontation. But I knew if you sat down and listened to her, you would understand." Aunt Clara placed her hand on Madeleine's shoulder again, and this time Madeleine left it there.

"I still think what she said to Mom was wrong," Madeleine said, a little sullen.

"But don't you feel so much better after forgiving her?"

"I do." Madeleine massaged her temples. "Just please never do that again."

"Okay. I will never invite your sworn enemy over for dinner again."

"Promise?" Madeleine stared intently into her aunt's eyes. Aunt Clara wasn't taking everything as seriously as Madeleine wished she would. "Promise," Aunt Clara said.

Satisfied, Madeleine nodded. Before she climbed into bed that night, she noticed an alert for a voice message. Her heart soared. Maybe A.J. called me! But the voice on the other end did not belong to A.J.

Hi, Maddy. It's your—

Madeleine quickly hung up. No. She wasn't ready to hear that voice.

And maybe she never would be.

* * *

"I thought you said it was over!"

"It was ... I thought it was."

Maddy covered her head with her pillow. She wanted to hear what her parents were saying, but she didn't want to hear at the same time. Something told her things were changing. Mom and Dad had been fighting for a long time now, but this was worse. She sensed the beginning of something. Or the end. She crept out of bed and cracked the door open.

"I can't believe I was so stupid!"

"No, you're not the stupid one. I am. I'm so sorry."

"No, I never should've trusted you again. Not after the first time."

Maddy's mother's voice rang out, loud and scarlet red. Her father's voice called back, sad and a soft, gray-blue. Dad had done something wrong. He was sorry, but Mom was very angry, too angry. Maddy quietly padded down the hallway, eager to hear better.

"Didn't you think I would see her number on the phone bill? Or the charges on the credit card?"

"Maybe I hoped you would." Dad's voice was small and scared. A pit of worry and uncertainty grew in Madeleine's belly.

"What is that supposed to mean?"

"I don't think I can do this anymore. I'm just not strong enough."

"I don't think I can either. Not if you don't get some help."

Maddy's heart dropped. She feared the worst. If there was a problem too big for her parents to fix, then it must be a terrible problem indeed.

"I've tried that. It didn't work."

"I found out about a group in Fayetteville. They have meetings as often as you need to go."

"I said, I tried that!" Dad's voice was angry now, but it broke.

"I'm just so tired. I'm so tired of being a terrible husband and a terrible father."

Maddy almost ran out of the hallway. Dad wasn't terrible. He was wonderful. He was the best dad in the whole world. Why would he say that?

"What do you want?" Mom sounded tired and sad, too. "Maybe I should leave. Maybe you'd be better off without me."

"You know that's not what I want. Henry! Look at me … You know that's not what I want, right?"

Maddy gasped for breath.

"Maddy? Sweetie?" Footsteps grew closer. Her mom came to her in the hallway. "Do you need something?"

"I … I need a drink of water." She was thirsty now that she thought of it. "Okay, Maddy, I'll be right there. You go back to bed now."

Maddy ran to her room, buried her face in her pillow, and pulled the covers tight around her. What would happen to them if Dad left? What would happen to her?

"Here's your water, sweetheart." Her mother knelt by the bed. "Is Dad going to leave us?"

"No, sweetie. He loves us very much." Mom combed Maddy's hair with her fingers.

"Why are you always fighting then?"

Maddy's mother sighed deeply. She rubbed her forehead. "Your father is going through some stuff. But he's going to be okay."

"Okay." Maddy wanted so badly for Mom to be right that she almost believed it.

"I love you, Mom." True, but Maddy only said it because she needed to hear her mom say it back.

"I love you, too, Maddy. I always have and I always will."

Maddy closed her eyes tight and tried not to hear her parents' muffled voices in the living room. Tried not to think about what might happen next.

a.J. stepped out of his truck into the bright sun. He hadn't always been a morning person, but after years of playing sports and now teaching and coaching, A.J. had gotten used to waking up early. He was accustomed to a relaxed schedule in the summer, but he was happy for the excuse to get out of the house on a beautiful Saturday morning, especially if it meant spending time with Madeleine.

He'd left the house even earlier than necessary to pick up half a dozen of his favorite donuts. The drive through the heart of Shady Springs and into the next town to get to the bakery took half an hour, but the smell wafting from the box in his hands told him it would be well worth the trip.

A.J. and Madeleine had been texting since Wednesday night, little messages to one another. "Good morning."

"How's it going?"

"You making any progress on those blobs of paint on the wall?"

Friday afternoon, Madeleine had asked if he wanted to come over for brunch. A.J. had suggested they go out, but Madeleine insisted on cooking. He'd hoped to bring her to the bakery, but bringing the bakery to her would be almost as good.

He rang the doorbell and heard a voice inside yelling, then quick pounding of feet to the front door. Madeleine swung open the door, out-of-breath but grinning. She was especially beautiful with her hair pulled up and a pink frilly apron tied around her waist. A smudge of flour marked her cheek and, before thinking, A.J. wiped it off with the pad of his thumb. A stunned expression crossed Madeleine's face.

"Good morning." A.J. held out the box of donuts almost as if it was a bouquet of flowers.

"Good morning!" Madeleine quickly recovered as her gaze fell on the bakery box. "What did you bring?"

"Only the best donuts in Arkansas. You're welcome." The smile on Madeleine's face reassured A.J. he'd definitely made the right move.

"Thank you! Come in!" Madeleine swept open the door and pulled
A.J. inside.

In the two years A.J. had known Clara, he'd never actually stepped foot in her house. They always met at school or church. As close as she lived to the high school, he'd simply never had a reason to come over. The house looked exactly as he'd imagined.

Morning light poured in from the large windows in the front room to his left and the dining room to his right. A large farmhouse table dominated the dining room and plush, overstuffed couches and armchairs furnished the long living room. A.J. peeked around the corner and found, as he'd suspected, bookshelves lined the back of the living room. Family portraits hung on the wall space not covered with books. Young Madeleine and her mother, a handsome man who must be George, and pictures that could only be young Clara. The overall effect was cozy and inviting. A.J. was instantly at ease in the home.

Directly in front of him was a stained oak staircase with a white banister. And down the hall was a spacious kitchen. Where smells of ... something ... wafted from the oven. Madeleine led him to the kitchen. A large window above the sink overlooked Clara's garden. Inside was a cozy breakfast nook and a small glass door leading to an enclosed sunroom.

As Madeleine set the box of donuts down, a smoke detector blared.

Madeleine cursed softly, then immediately apologized. "I'm so sorry. I didn't mean to say that." She looked around frantically before pulling a chair over to the source of the noise.

"Allow me." A.J. only had to lift up on his toes slightly to reach the button. Perks of being tall. "There."

"Thanks. I guess the muffins are done." Madeleine pulled a pan of half-burnt muffins out of the oven and set them on the stove next to a pot of scrambled eggs and a plate of very crispy bacon.

"I promise I've cooked before." Madeleine sighed. "I guess I got distracted and forgot to set a timer."

"Well, I don't think this is bad. Trust me, even after living by myself for three years, I'm still learning how to cook."

Madeleine took off her oven mitts and poked at the muffins. "I can probably save the tops of these. That's the best part, anyway, right?"

"Everything okay?" Clara poked her head down from the top of the stairs. "Hello, A.J."

"Hello, Clara. Just a little smoke. Nothing we can't fix." He gave her a thumbs up.

"All right. I've already eaten, so I'll leave you two in peace."

Madeleine's eyes widened. "Really? I thought you were going to join us. How in the world are A.J. and I going to eat all this food?"

"Oh, I think A.J. can handle himself. Holler if you need me!" Clara retreated upstairs, and A.J. and Madeleine were left alone in the kitchen. "I promise I didn't invite you over to trick you into a date or anything." Her cheeks glowed a bright red, and she fiddled with the oven mitts.

"That's okay. I don't mind." He liked that Madeleine thought of them hanging out as a date. Even the possibility made him smile before he mentally kicked himself. We're only friends, nothing more.

"It's just, Aunt Clara is very pushy when it comes to setting people up ... as you might remember."

"Don't worry." He waved his hands. "No assumptions here. I just came for the food."

"Good. Great." Madeleine sliced off the tops of the muffins in the tin and piled them into a breadbasket. She set the basket, the plate of bacon, and the box of donuts on the small kitchen table. Then she spooned the scrambled eggs into a big bowl and sprinkled a handful of cheese on top.

A.J. surreptitiously checked to make sure the oven and every burner were turned off. Better safe than sorry.

"I know you don't like coffee, but would you like some juice or milk?"

"Milk would be great."

Madeleine moved through the kitchen, pulling plates and cups from the cupboard and pouring drinks for each of them. A.J. watched helplessly as she made all the preparations. He was so used to doing everything for himself, he struggled watching Madeleine work so hard on his behalf. He mentally made a note to do the dishes after they finished eating.

Finally, Madeleine and A.J. sat down to eat. They piled their plates with the steaming food. Burnt muffins aside, everything actually looked pretty good. Once they were ready to eat, A.J. offered to bless the food.

"God, thank You for this beautiful Saturday morning and the delicious meal Madeleine has prepared. May we praise You in everything we do. In Jesus's name we pray, Amen."

"Thanks. You didn't have to call the food delicious. I'm sure God doesn't appreciate your sarcasm."

"Actually, it wasn't sarcastic." A.J. swallowed the eggs in his mouth before stabbing another forkful. "These eggs are amazing. How do you get them so fluffy?"

"You cook them low and slow. Also, I added a little butter and cream.

That helps." Madeleine smiled shyly.

A.J. was pleased to have flattered her. "Mmm. You'll have to show me sometime."

"Only if you promise to show me where you got these donuts." Madeleine held up a half-eaten chocolate one.

"Deal." A.J. bit into a glazed one himself. It was sugary and pillow- soft, and somehow, still slightly warm. Best donuts ever.

"I see you share in the family curse." Madeleine wiped the chocolate crumbs off her face.

"What's that?" A.J. dabbed at his own mouth. "An insatiable love of sweets."

"Ah, yes. I suppose I do." A.J. thought over all of the dessert he'd eaten with Madeleine recently. Ice cream, shave ice, milkshakes, and now donuts. Maybe he needed to cut back a little.

"I don't usually eat this much sugar," Madeleine said. "At home, Mom never makes dessert or keeps any junk food in the house. We're both terrible about eating too many sweets. Aunt Clara isn't much better."

"That's probably for the best, then. I know my bad habits will catch up to me someday." A.J. patted his middle. "My dad has developed quite the gut, and I know I will too in a few more years."

"Really?" Madeleine laughed. "I don't think I can imagine you overweight."

"Imagine me overweight with a mustache and gray hair and that's my dad."

Madeleine's eyes crinkled in delight. He could listen to her laugh all day. "I can't imagine you with a mustache either." She paused to take a breath. "Are you very much like your dad? On the inside?"

"No, not at all. I'm exactly like my mom. That's what makes my name so ironic."

Madeleine furrowed her eyebrows in question. Right. She didn't know his full name.

"Didn't you ever wonder what A.J. stands for?" Most people asked right away.

"I didn't want to pry." She cocked her head, expectant.

"Arthur Junior. Named after my father." A.J. shrugged. He was reminded again of how ridiculous that was. He was only a junior in looks. In every other way, he was completely different from his father.

"Arthur. Sorry, it doesn't quite suit you." The hint of a smile touched Madeleine's lips.

"I agree. And so does my family. Hence, the nickname." His younger sisters hadn't been able to pronounce Arthur, and his parents saw the stark difference in personality at a young age, so his mom came up with

A.J. and the name had stuck since then.

"If you're nothing like your dad, what is he like?" She rested her elbows on the table.

"He's very disappointed in me." He smirked, shaking his head. Madeleine raised her eyebrows.

"Well, not very disappointed. But definitely a little disappointed." He took a drink of his milk.

"Why?" A confused expression spread across her face, and A.J. wanted nothing more than to reach over and straighten out the wrinkle in her brow. He shook his head, trying to remember his train of thought.

"He wanted me to go into business like him. Finance or accounting, something like that. Something practical. But I just couldn't sit still long enough. I tried all sorts of different majors before settling on a history degree with teaching certification."

"Like what? What did you try?" Madeleine asked, her expression intrigued.

"Oh, biology, music, math, Bible ..." His dad had been angry about all of the wasted hours of study. Thankfully, A.J. had been able to use most of his classes toward general education requirements and a minor in ministry.

"Wow." Her eyebrows shot up. "That is a lot. It must be nice to be good at so many different things."

"I wouldn't say I'm good at all of them ... but, yes. I enjoy a wide range of topics and disciplines. That's why I like teaching. I get to work out my energy in the classroom and on the track. And I get to use my random knowledge of lots of subjects while teaching history."

"You're a gifted speaker. I've been meaning to tell you that. I loved your lesson on Wednesday night."

"Thanks. You'll have to come back sometime." A.J. reached over and punched her shoulder teasingly.

"I'd like that." Madeleine pursed her lips in a contemplative frown. "Have you ever thought about being a preacher?"

He had, a long time ago, but he'd never imagined himself qualified for such a job. "Don't you have to be at least fifty? I'm not sure if I have the gravitas to be a preacher."

"I think you'd be great." Her expression turned serious. "Speaking of church, I have something to tell you."

"Hmm?" A.J. tried to keep a neutral expression on his face as he shoved some more donut in his mouth. He hoped this would be the moment she shared her desire to become a Christian.

"Nancy Jones came over last night."

A.J. spewed out half his bite of donut and began choking on the other half. He drank a huge gulp of milk. Then he grabbed a wad of napkins to clean up. After the coughing had subsided, A.J. cleared his throat. "How did that go?"

"Are you okay?" A mixture of worry and amusement passed over her face.

"Yeah, I'm fine." He waved off her concern. "What happened last night?"

She shrugged. "Aunt Clara invited her over for dinner without telling me, which was not very nice of her. But we talked. And I forgave her."

"Wow. That's awesome. That's ... that's really awesome."

"Yeah. It is." Madeleine nodded. "I know it'll take a while for me to really let everything go, but I'm starting to, and it feels great."

A.J. smiled. In only a little over a week, Madeleine had already changed from the bitter, sensitive girl he first met.

They continued to talk about Madeleine's mural, about their favorite donut flavors, and the pros and cons of coffee drinking. A.J. helped rinse dishes in the sink and sat with Madeleine in the living room until he checked the clock and realized it was well past time for lunch. Not that he was hungry. He just didn't want to overstay his welcome.

"I'd better head out. Thank you for the food." A.J stood and waited, awkwardly, for a moment, then decided to go in for a hug from the side. Madeleine, surprised, let out a little "Oh!" then patted him on the shoulder. The hug was perhaps the weirdest he'd ever given, but Madeleine didn't act like she minded, smiling instead.

He ducked his head then turned to her. "I had fun. I'm really glad you came to Shady Springs."

"Me, too." And for the first time, A.J. actually believed Madeleine wanted to be here, with him and in Shady Springs, with her whole heart.

18

*L*ater that afternoon, Madeleine was folding clothes upstairs when she heard a car door slam. At that moment, Aunt Clara was in the backyard working in the garden. Madeleine didn't remember her mentioning expecting a visitor, but after last night's surprise guest, she didn't know what to expect from Aunt Clara.

Curious, Madeleine peeked through the window and immediately dropped to the floor. She forced herself up again to double-check. Surely not. She must have seen wrong. The man outside was just someone who looked like him.

But no. There was the same curly hair, the same slight slump to the shoulders, he even had a plaid shirt and brown shoes like he always used to wear.

Her father.

Madeleine sat on the bed, heart racing. She pressed her fingers to her forehead and tried to concentrate. I have to get out of here. She threw the freshly laundered clothes into her suitcase and grabbed everything she could fit in her arms from the bathroom. She whispered a prayer of thanks that her art supplies were still in their bag from yesterday. Whatever I forget to pack, I can buy when I get home.

Bags in hand, Madeleine flew down the stairs. The doorbell rang.

She froze. Should she slip out the side door and drive away? Aunt Clara was right—Madeleine was afraid of confrontation. But a small, quiet voice inside of her whispered, Don't you want to see him? Haven't you imagined this moment a million times?

Slowly, Madeleine walked down the hallway toward the door. Too slowly, apparently, and the doorbell rang again. At long last, Madeleine reached the door and pulled it open with trembling hands.

"Madeleine?"

The man at the door was certainly her father, but Madeleine was shocked by how different he looked. His hair was still thick and curly, but gray was sprinkled in with the brown. He had the same kind face, but fine lines fanned out from his eyes and mouth. He seemed shorter, too, but maybe that was Madeleine's fault. She was much taller than the last time she'd seen him.

"Dad." Madeleine took a deep breath, trying to remember everything she wanted to say to him. Her mind was blank. There was too much and not enough in her head all at once. Questions flew by but none within grasp. This was not going the way she'd always envisioned.

"Henry?" Aunt Clara stood behind Madeleine.

"How could you?" Instead of directing any of the million questions she had toward her father, Madeleine turned on her aunt. "How could you invite him here? After everything? After promising to never do that to me again?"

"Madeleine, I—" Aunt Clara shook her head, mouth hanging open. "No." Madeleine marched out the open door with her bags, shoving her father aside. Her pulse raced as she threw her things in the car. "Madeleine, please. I didn't—" Clara ran to catch up.

"I can't do this again. I'm going back to Kansas City. I'm going home."

"What about the mural?"

"I don't know. I'll call Sam. We'll figure something out." She slammed the car door.

In a moment of poetic beauty, the road was clear, and Madeleine peeled out of the driveway, past her father's car and a gaping Aunt Clara, onto the street and out of Shady Springs.

The drive home was four hours, and Madeleine's red-hot fury fueled her for about an hour of that trip. She fumed about the audacity of her aunt inviting unwanted visitors not once, but twice. Who would do something like that? Aunt Clara, that's who. She was always meddlesome, but becoming a widow had only made her worse.

Then she fumed about her father. All summer, he'd been emailing and calling. Why now? Why did he choose this summer to contact her? Why did he skip out on all her teenage years, when she desperately needed him, only to return now that she was grown and in her twenties?

She found herself wanting to talk out loud to someone. Who? Her mom? Not yet. A.J.? She was afraid he wouldn't understand. She almost didn't even dare ask herself. God? Was she wanting to talk to God?

The gas light blinked on, and Madeleine searched for the closest station. Just in time, too. She was reaching the end of her anger as well as the end of her gasoline. Now, sadness crept in, indigo and gray. Sorrow washed over her as she slumped in her seat. She pushed her palms against her eyes and tried to breathe deeply to keep from crying. Exhausted, Madeleine climbed out of the car to fill up.

She thought about calling her mom to let her know she was on her way but texted instead. Madeleine wasn't sure how her mother would react, or what floodgates the conversation would open within herself, and she wasn't in the mood to get into everything with her mom yet. Once in the car again, Madeleine drove at a more reasonable speed and listened to the radio and some soft rock to get through the rest of the drive.

To her credit, Madeleine's mother did not ask questions. She simply greeted Madeleine at the door with a cup of tea and some help unpacking her bags. For dinner, they ordered out from the vegetarian place they both loved. They split a big bowl of Madeleine's favorite tofu and mushroom salad and went to bed early, ignoring all calls and texts, although Madeleine did notice her mother eyeing her own phone. Aunt Clara must have moved on to her sister, realizing her niece was not going to answer.

The next morning, Madeleine's mother only briefly asked, "Anything you want to talk about?"

"No."

"Okay … I'm here if you do … want to talk."

Madeleine went for a jog and then packed an order from her website to ship off at the post office the next day. In the afternoon, she picked up a few hours at the restaurant, even though today was Sunday—her least favorite day to wait tables. And that evening after work, Madeleine decided to get together with friends.

What would everyone think when they didn't see her at church? She brushed off the thought. Let them wonder.

Madeleine did take the time to call Sam that night. She fumbled over the digits, wishing that she could just send him a text. "Hello, Sam? It's Madeleine Mullins."

"Madeleine. We missed you at worship this morning. How are you?"

"Fine." The answer was automatic, although she was not actually fine. "I needed to come home to Kansas City for a few days."

"Is everything all right?"

How could she possibly respond? "I'm very sorry for the inconvenience."

"That's okay."

"I'll be in touch." She went to end the call but added at the last minute, "Thanks for everything, Sam." She didn't know when or if she'd ever return to Shady Springs, but she'd bought herself some time. Madeleine needed the money even more than before, and she couldn't afford to disappoint a client. But the thought of going back made her pulse race and her stomach churn.

She sat down to draw, but nothing would come to her. The only image in her head was her father standing in Aunt Clara's doorway. Even working with clay, her foolproof method for getting out of a creative funk, failed her.

The next several days passed like that. Working, spending time with friends, attempting to draw or paint. Madeleine blocked out all thoughts of Shady Springs and her father, except when an occasional text from

A.J. would come through.

A.J.: How's it going?

A.J.: Don't forget, u still have to go to that donut shop with me. But after a few days, even the texts from A.J. stopped.

* * *

A.J. paced the floor of Sam's office. There wasn't a lot of space, so walking from one side to the other only took him a couple seconds.

Sam cleared his throat. "Tell me exactly what's bothering you. And try not to knock anything off the shelf, please."

A.J. kept his arms from swinging by hooking his thumbs in the belt loops of his blue jeans. "Madeleine hasn't answered any texts or calls from me—or Clara—for almost a week." He tried to stand still but could only manage it for a moment before his feet took off again. "We spent the morning together on Saturday, and then I heard nothing else from her the rest of the weekend. I found out from Clara at church on Sunday that Madeleine's dad showed up out of the blue. But that doesn't explain why she disappeared." A.J. stopped suddenly and pivoted to face Sam. "What about the mural? Have you heard anything from her? Doesn't she have to come back?"

"I spoke with her last week. She's in Kansas City, but I don't know for how long. Technically, she doesn't have to come back. We just have a spoken agreement, no contract. But if she doesn't return, we will have to paint the wall gray again." Sam shrugged and pursed his lips.

"Paint over it? But she worked so hard. Couldn't we find someone to finish the mural?" A.J. had been looking forward to seeing the completed painting. Some color would've really livened up the space, and the mural might have even been a point of conversation.

"Who do you recommend exactly?" Sam raised an eyebrow, resting his chin on folded hands. When A.J. didn't answer, he continued. "I'm disappointed, too. Madeleine seemed like an answer to prayer. She needed the money, we liked her art, and Clara thought it would be a good opportunity for her to spend time with Christians." He sighed and shook his head. "It would seem she simply wasn't committed to following through."

Finally tired of his pacing, A.J. plopped down in the chair opposite Sam. "It's not like her to flake out like this." At least, he didn't think it was. He didn't know Madeleine that well, but from what he'd seen, she was a responsible person who valued loyalty and integrity. "I think she must have been really hurt in order to leave like this, with a job unfinished."

Sam gave a small smile. "I hope she returns. I pray she does, but in the meantime, we need to give her space. We can't force her to come to Shady Springs ... or to Jesus. That's something she has to decide for herself."

A.J. nodded. "I just hope she makes the right choice."

19

*O*n Friday night, almost a week after Madeleine had come home to Kansas City, her mother found her sitting on her bed.

Madeleine quickly tucked her phone under her leg to hide the fact that she'd been reading through her texts from A.J. one more time, wishing things had been different.

"I need to tell you something." Madeleine's mother sat down at the desk across from her. The room was small, so their knees practically touched. "I've been talking to Aunt Clara."

"I figured you would." Madeleine wasn't too upset about that. They were sisters, after all, and they'd always been close. "Did she tell you what she did? How she and Dad ambushed me?"

"That's what I need to tell you." Catherine took a deep breath. "I told your father where you were, not Clara."

"What?" Madeleine involuntarily scooted back several inches on her bed and away from her mother. This was possibly the last thing she'd thought her mom would say.

"He'd been calling me, so I talked to him." Catherine rubbed her forehead. "I didn't think he would just show up unannounced."

Madeleine stared down at the bedspread, shaking her head. "Madeleine, he's your father. Doesn't a part of you want to talk to him, after all these years?"

"Of course, I do!" Madeleine exploded. "But I want to do it on my terms. I don't want to be forced into talking to him."

"Would you have done it? Would you have ever worked up the nerve to talk to him? He told me he'd been leaving emails and voice messages for you, and that you hadn't answered any."

"He was gone for ten years. Surely he can wait a few months for me to answer his emails." Madeleine stood and retreated to the corner of the room, her arms crossed, her cheeks warm. "How dare you. All I've ever done is support you while you wallow in grief and work. What gives you the right to do this to me? The both of you. To take my father away and bring him back again just as suddenly."

Madeleine's mother flinched, mouth open as if she'd been slapped. A twinge of guilt twisted in Madeleine's gut, but her words were already out of her mouth, hanging in the air between them. Although her anger dissipated a little, she couldn't deny the truth of what she'd said.

"Did you ever think that maybe I don't want you to turn out like me? That maybe wallowing in grief and work is not healthy?" Her mom hung her head, her voice defeated.

"I'm twenty-two years old! I'm not a child anymore. You can't force me to forgive him. You can't control me." Madeleine was through with people meddling in her life. First, Aunt Clara and now her mother. Enough was enough.

"Don't you see where this is headed?" Catherine's eyes shone with sorrow and pity. "If you can't forgive him, if you can't at least talk to him, you're never going to heal."

"Maybe I don't want to heal." Madeleine's voice sounded petulant and immature, but she didn't care.

"That's … that's stupid." Catherine threw up her hands. "Of course, you want to heal. And so do I. That's why I'm trying to mend things with your dad."

"Well, fine. Go ahead and invite him to move in with us!" Madeleine yelled.

"What? No. I'm not … we're not talking like that. I need to … I've been carrying this weight for so long." Catherine massaged her forehead. "This hurt and anger and self-hatred. When Henry called, I just … I saw the chance to unload that burden. And I took it."

Madeleine walked to her mother and put her arms around her. Catherine's resignation broke through Madeleine's feverish anger. Did she really want to burn bridges with her entire family over this? She recognized her mother's quiet desperation. It was the same she carried inside herself.

"I talked to Nancy Jones. The day before Dad showed up, Aunt Clara invited her over for dinner." She sat on the bed. "It went really well, surprisingly. I never knew she was so close to Dad. You're right. It did feel like a burden being lifted."

Catherine lowered her gaze. "There are so many things I never should have told you."

"But I heard Nancy talking to you. That wasn't your fault."

Catherine waved her hands, dismissing her argument. "I know, but I could've handled it better. You shouldn't have had to share the burden of that grudge. That was mine to bear."

"Have you forgiven Nancy?" Madeleine searched her mother's eyes. "You know, I'm not happy with the woman. But …" She nodded slowly. "I think I've let it go. And I think if you could forgive Nancy, you could at least talk to your father." Madeleine's mother raised her eyebrows, an unspoken question on her face.

"No, I don't know. I mean … maybe." She shook her head. "Maybe someday I can forgive him."

"Have a conversation with him, sweetie. You don't have to forgive him."

"I think I do." Madeleine paused, weighing her words. Should she tell Mom? About reading the Bible? About all of her questions?

"Take your time." She stood, placing her hands on Madeleine's shoulders. "I'm sorry that everything happened the way it did."

"You should have just talked to me."

Catherine nodded. "You're right. I'm sorry. I never meant to rush you. But I think you should talk to him."

"I will."

Her mom left, quietly closing the door. And Madeleine crawled into her bed, curled up around her bent legs, and prayed. God ... Madeleine struggled for what to say. How could she possibly put into words everything that was inside of her? Then she remembered something Aunt Clara had told her—God knows what you need and what you're going to say even before you say it. God, You know what is best. You know what I'm feeling. God ... please help me.

* * *

Maddy's world was falling apart. "You don't have to do this, Dad."

"I do, Maddy. I hope someday you'll understand."

Maddy grabbed at her father, holding on as tight as she could. "Please don't go," she said into his jacket.

"I wish I didn't have to. I promise it's for your own good."

"How?"

Maddy's father pulled back to stare into her eyes. "I'm not ... I'm not good to be around right now. I don't want to hurt you any more than I already have."

But how could he possibly hurt her more than this?

He pulled something from his jacket. A letter, pages and pages, filling up an envelope. "Give this to Mom, okay?"

"Okay."

"I'll call soon. I promise."

"I love you, Daddy."

"I love you, too, Maddy-Maddy-Bo-Baddy."

For the very last time, Maddy hugged her father. He shook in her arms. His cheeks were wet against hers. Then he pried himself from her grip and drove away in his little red car.

Maddy closed her eyes tight. She seared the memory of his hazel eyes, the smell of his spearmint gum, his scratchy face into her mind. She didn't know when she would see him next, and she never wanted to forget how much she loved her Daddy.

20

*T*he next day was Saturday, and Madeleine continued her routine. Staring at an empty sketchbook in the morning, waiting tables in the afternoon. But instead of going out with friends that night, she stayed in. Her mom was working a weekend shift, and Madeleine had the whole house to herself. She picked up an order of sesame noodles at the Chinese place on the way home and briefly debated binge-watching a TV show, but somehow ended up in her mom's closet instead.

All the talk about her dad and what happened made Madeleine wonder if there weren't any photos her mother had kept. Madeleine had two herself, but surely Mom had old pictures she'd stored away. If she could look through them again, maybe she would be able to remember why she needed to forgive her father in the first place.

Madeleine went straight to the back of the closet, not wasting any time sorting through the crates marked "Tax Files" or "Madeleine Art K-5." A few unlabeled boxes on the top shelf appeared a little older than the rest, and she pulled the closest one down.

And there he was. Madeleine's breath caught in her throat.

Young Dad with a young Mom on their wedding day. Engagement pictures. A newspaper announcement. Madeleine searched their faces for some clue to the problems threatening their marriage ahead, but they smiled blissfully. Two worry-free twenty-somethings. Happy and in love.

Then came the baby pictures. Madeleine had been born before the dawn of social media and selfies, so most of the photos were of Madeleine and her mother, but a few showed a smiling Henry. He hadn't been much older than Madeleine was when he'd become a father. Twenty-four. Her parents hadn't been considered too young to be parents, although Madeleine certainly did not feel ready for kids. Maybe her dad hadn't been ready either.

Madeleine continued to leaf through photos. Opening day of Dad's portrait studio. A picnic in Spring Park. A day at the lake. A parade. Madeleine's first art show. Memories flooded in that Madeleine hadn't thought about in years. She had such a hard time reconciling the father from the pictures with the father who sunk into alcoholism and adultery and left his family for ten years.

At the end of the first box, Madeleine reached to the back of the shelf for another. The box almost came crashing down on top of her. She hadn't expected it to be so heavy. Much heavier than the first. When Madeleine opened it up, she saw why. It was filled with her old books. And at the top of the box was a Study Bible her mom had bought for her when she turned ten. Her name was engraved on the front in silver, swooping letters, though that was concealed by the ridiculous Bible cover she'd stuffed it in.

Madeleine cleaned up the boxes but took the Bible to her room. She'd never finished Matthew and had left Sam's Bible at Aunt Clara's house in her rush to leave. Now, she turned to where she'd left off in chapter 26.

Madeleine had heard the story of the death of Jesus many

times and in many different ways. But as she turned through the pages of her childhood Bible and reread the story through a new lens, one colored with the yellow green brightness of her summer with A.J. and the rosy red of her warm conversations with Clara and Nancy and also the black of her newly exposed wounds, Madeleine saw a whole new story.

She saw a God who loved her so much He came down to live as a human. A God who was betrayed at every level, even by those who claimed to love Him the most. A God who willingly died in the most horrible way possible. And a God who defeated death. A God who suffered all of those things in order to save humanity from itself.

As Madeleine read, her heart raced. What did I do to deserve this? What did any of us do to deserve this? I can't even work up the goodwill to talk to my own father. Why would God want to save me?

Finally, as Madeleine reached the end of the book and Jesus was speaking to His followers, she read the words, "Go and make disciples of all nations, baptizing them in the name of the Father and of the Son and of the Holy Spirit, and teaching them to obey everything I have commanded you. And surely, I am with you always, to the very end of the age."

She bent her head in shame and humility. God, I don't know why You would do everything You did, but I believe now that You did it. I don't deserve Your love, but You gave it to me. What do You want me to do now?

Madeleine opened her eyes, and one thought shouted in her mind. I need to follow Jesus. I need to call A.J.

"Hello?" He picked up on the first ring. That must mean he wasn't too angry at her for leaving.

"A.J., I want to get baptized."

"Okay. Great! Wow." His voice on the other end carried the same excitement in her own heart.

"I want you to do it. I want you to baptize me." She stood and paced the room, energy coursing through her body.

"I'd be honored. Are you sure you're ready? The last time we talked, you had some serious doubts." He paused on the other end of the line. "Are you all right, Madeleine? I haven't heard from you, and I was worried."

Madeleine bit her lip. She was torn up inside to think that she'd hurt him and Aunt Clara and Sam. "I know, A.J. I'm sorry about how I left. You didn't deserve to be treated that way." Her feet came to a halt. "But I think that's why I have to get baptized now. I have to start making changes. I don't think I've ever felt more sure about anything. I want to become a Christian—I know this is what I need to do."

"I have to be here for church tomorrow, but I could come after morning services."

"No. I'm coming to Shady Springs. Right now. Meet me at the church building at ..." Madeleine checked at the clock and added four hours. "At eleven-thirty. Sorry, I know that's late."

"Don't worry about it, Madeleine. I'll be there."

"Are you sure?"

"You're right. This can't wait."

They talked a few more minutes. A.J. guided her through what would happen when she got baptized. Madeleine caught her reflection in her bedroom mirror as she disconnected the call. Her hair was a mess, but she was grinning like a fool. She hadn't been this excited in ... never. She had never been this excited and peaceful and joyful all at the same time.

Years ago, before everything that happened with Madeleine's parents, she had been very close to taking on Christ. She'd been studying with her Bible class teachers and praying hard about the decision to get baptized. If things had gone differently ... Well, there was no use in wondering what might have happened. Madeleine needed to change her life—starting right now.

She typed a message to her mom.

Madeleine: I'm driving to Shady Springs. Nothing's wrong. In fact, everything is really good. I need to finish what I started. I love you.

She set the phone on her desk and grabbed her suitcase. She needed to pack enough clothes to get her through the weekend. And to finish the mural like she promised. She was loading up the car when her mom pulled up to the house, home from her shift.

"Don't leave yet." Catherine parked her car and ran toward the front door.

"Did you get my text? I'm going to Arkansas!"

"Wait for me!" her mother called before she let the door swing shut.

A few minutes later, Catherine appeared with a bag of her own. "I'm coming with you."

"I'm going to Shady Springs. I want to get baptized."

"I know. I'm coming with you." Her mother's eyes shone with determination.

"Don't you have to work?"

"I'm off tomorrow, and I can take a sick day on Monday if I need to."

"But you'll be at church. In Shady Springs."

"I know. It's time for me to go back, too." She climbed into the passenger seat and that was that.

The drive to Arkansas flew by. They passed the time by singing and talking and laughing. Madeleine caught herself staring at her mother in the passenger seat. The woman next to her was carefree and unburdened. She was content. Madeleine shook her head. If only she'd known sooner how much they both needed to confront the problems of their past. If only she'd known how much happier her mother could be.

Madeleine had a lot to make up for. She'd left everyone in the lurch when she took off. She'd blamed Aunt Clara for her dad's reappearance, something that was not her fault. And she'd betrayed all of the other friendships she had built over her time in Shady Springs. She'd left A.J. and Sam and Sophie and Caitlin, everybody, without so much as a goodbye.

But she was ready to start over. Maybe they'd never forgive her, but she had to try. If nothing else, she knew she would have the forgiveness of God.

As Madeleine rolled down the highway and pulled into the church parking lot, she was shocked to see about twenty cars. What in the world? She'd expected A.J.'s car and maybe Clara's or Sam's. What were all these people doing here at almost midnight? Maybe there was a youth event or church camp or something.

But as Madeleine walked into the auditorium, she saw that it was full of people. Everyone she'd abandoned. Nancy, Sam, Julie, Sophie, Caitlin, Jessica, Phoebe, even Mitchell and Dylan. And Clara, her beautiful, strong aunt who had stuck with her through everything.

A knot tightened in Madeleine's throat. She tried to talk but choked on the overwhelming emotions coursing through her. Aunt Clara enveloped her in a hug, and all of Madeleine's pent-up feelings broke loose.

"I'm so sorry for everything," she said into her aunt's shoulder. "I'm so sorry, everyone," she said louder, turning to the crowd. "I let you all down. I was selfish and downright cold with some of you. It means so much to me that you came."

"We'll have enough time for speeches later. Let's get you baptized."

A.J. hugged her shoulders, then led her to the front of the auditorium. Aunt Clara embraced her sister, and they walked together to the very first pew.

Madeleine stood in the water, gazing out at all of her friends —no— family. Her church family. And she knew she was completely loved. Every last one of them was broken and sinful, but they were beautiful to her. These people loved God, and they loved each other. They certainly weren't perfect, but they were family.

"Madeleine would like to share her confession."

Madeleine had listened to many others make this same confession of faith, but she believed the words to be the truest she'd ever said.

"I believe that Jesus Christ is the Son of God."

"I now baptize you in the name of the Father, the Son, and the Holy Spirit."

A.J. held her head securely and dipped her back. The water closed over her, burying her old self with its bitter and fearful heart. She rose out a new person, carrying not the weight of her anger but the forgiveness of her God.

21

*M*adeleine reached for the door and pulled her hand back again. She paced the sidewalk outside Mike's Diner once

more. She reached for the handle a second time. This was a mistake. Finally, she mustered enough courage to open the door and marched through, forcing her body forward.

He wasn't here yet. Of course not. He'd always been late for everything. Why wouldn't he be late for the long-awaited reunion with his only child?

No, wait. There he was. Madeleine just hadn't recognized his head of graying hair.

"Dad."

Her father stood quickly. His arms twitched like they wanted to wrap themselves around her, but she made no move to reciprocate. Instead, she sat.

"Have you ordered anything?" she asked.

"Um, no. Not yet." He gave a cursory glance at the menu then turned his gaze to her.

Madeleine skimmed over a list of milkshake flavors propped up on the table, although she was suddenly queasy.

"How are you?" he asked.

"Fine." Madeleine looked around for a waitress before remembering she'd need to go up to the counter. "Would you like to order something?"

"Yeah, sure."

They stood and strode over to the counter, Madeleine walking ahead so she wouldn't have to make eye contact with her father.

"I'll have a small chocolate milkshake and a small fry." Madeleine pulled out her wallet, but her father waved it away.

"I'm buying." Then turning to the woman behind the counter, he said, "I'll have the same thing."

At their table with nothing between them but a plastic number for their order, Madeleine finally glanced up at her father.

"Thanks for agreeing to meet," he said, wringing his hands a little before laying them flat on the table.

Madeleine's gaze roamed around the restaurant, observing the other patrons. She was thankful not to recognize anyone there, an unusual occurrence in such a small town.

"I wanted to start by saying how sorry I am." His fingers twitched again, reaching toward hers. She moved her hands to her lap. "You'll never know how truly sorry I am. For everything."

"So that's what you came here to say?" Madeleine pressed her lips together.

"No. I mean—Yes." He let out a breath. "But what I really want is to have a relationship with you."

"You did have a relationship with me." She crossed her arms. "A pretty good one, as I recall."

"The best, Maddy." He smiled softly.

"So why did you leave?" Madeleine narrowed her eyes.

"You know why. I was cheating on your mom. I was an alcoholic." He said the words matter-of-factly, as if he'd rehearsed them many times. But those truths weighed heavy in the air between them.

"But, why? Why did you do those things when you had such a great life here, with us?" Madeleine had never understood how anyone could throw away a family and a happy life.

"I was depressed—I have depression. I just didn't know it then. Your mom tried to get me help." He shook his head, running his hands through his hair.

"I remember." She thought back to all of the late-night conversations she'd overheard from the hallway.

"I was too stubborn and too deep within myself, within my sadness, to see a way out. I didn't even know what kind of help to get. My therapist tells me I was self-medicating by drinking, which made everything worse." His head drooped a little, and Madeleine recognized something in the defeated expression he wore. There was a side of her father she remembered all too well.

"What happened?" She leaned forward, placing her hands on the table. "You stopped calling and never visited. What happened to you?"

A waitress came by with their fries and milkshakes. Madeleine sipped her shake then set it aside.

"For a little while, I thought maybe I could fix everything on my own." He fumbled with his straw. "Then I thought I could make things work with … the other woman."

Madeleine winced. The thought of her dad with anyone other than her mom still grossed her out.

"What I found out is that I carried the same baggage no matter who I was with, except the next time it was even easier to leave."

He'd left the other woman. Madeleine had always wondered about that, afraid her father had a second family with children and a wife he loved more.

"What did you do then?" Madeleine twirled her straw

wrapper around her fingers. She'd told herself over and over that it didn't matter why he left and why he stayed away, but she still wanted to know, as if knowing why might soften the blow somehow.

"I floated around awhile, taking pictures, drinking too much, and my work suffered." He lowered his gaze to his cup, stirring his shake with the straw. "Then I hit my lowest point. I won't go into details, but things were really rough for a while. And it was at a men's home that I found God again."

"How long ago was that?"

He studied his hands on the table. "Three years."

"Three years?" Madeleine fought to keep her voice down, checking that no one was listening. "You've been sober for three years and you're just now reaching out?"

"I know, Maddy." His eyes were sorrowful. "I've been sober for three years, but I only recently got up the courage to come find you. I knew you would be angry, and I knew I didn't have a good enough excuse for leaving."

Madeleine picked up a fry and set it down again. She squinted against the sunlight as another customer walked in.

"I called once when you graduated from high school. And I went to George's funeral." He moved his glass around on the table. "I sat at the back so no one would see me, although I think your aunt might've. George was a good man. I'm sorry I didn't get to spend more time with him."

Madeleine nodded. She didn't want to talk about Uncle George with him. She didn't want to discuss the man who'd been like a father to her with the man who wasn't brave enough to take responsibility and be her father.

"A few months after that, I checked into the men's home. Once I graduated, I was able to work again. I lived in Little Rock for two years, and then I moved to Fayetteville a little while ago. I even have my own company." He beamed. "When I found out you were here in Shady Springs, I had to come see you. I couldn't wait any longer."

Madeleine's father reached across the table and placed his hand on her shoulder. Madeleine risked a glance into his eyes and found they were glistening but full of joy. Something inside of her broke. She hadn't thought her heart had room for anything but hatred for this man, but here she was feeling pity for him.

"I am so sorry I didn't call or visit. I wasted so much time. I missed everything. But I'm glad I got to see you again." His voice rang with sincerity. He rubbed her shoulder a bit before folding his hands on the table.

"Me, too." Madeleine hadn't expected to be moved by his story. She'd set up this meeting to work toward reconciliation ... eventually. She never thought she'd be ready to make amends this quickly.

Her heart hadn't truly forgotten how to love him. Maybe the reason she had so much anger toward him was because she needed all of that fury to quell the hurt of being separated. He would always be her daddy. "Thank you for sharing that with me." She rocked a little in her seat.

"I'm glad you're here."

"Me, too, sweetie." He smiled, and Madeleine could see something of the man from those old photos in Mom's closet. She returned his smile.

Madeleine and her father both stared at their food as if seeing it for the first time.

"Do you still dip your fries in your milkshake?" He observed her as if she were a stranger. She probably looked that way to him. Older, taller. He would have no idea what kind of music she liked or what her friends' names were. But maybe some things hadn't changed.

"Yeah, I do." And just to prove it, she dipped the warm, salty fry into the cool, sweet chocolate. Perfect.

They sat there in a not unpleasant silence, eating. Finally,

Madeleine threw away their trash and grabbed her purse. "I'd like to meet again, if that's okay."

She hadn't known quite what to expect going into this afternoon, but now she knew. She wasn't returning to the way things were before. Not the way things were before he left, and not the way things were after he left, but a new way. A new relationship borne out of the struggles they'd both had and the years apart, but also the shared love they had for each other. A love that hadn't dimmed, not even a little bit.

"I'd like that a lot, Maddy-Maddy-Bo-Baddy." Madeleine nodded as if to say, Yes, this is okay.

When they reached the parking lot, Madeleine turned to say goodbye. Before even thinking about what she was doing, she grabbed her father in a hug. Even ten years later, he smelled exactly the same, like cologne and spearmint gum.

"I love you, Daddy." Madeleine pulled back but kept a hand on each

of his arms. "I want to forgive you. It might take me a long time, but I'm going to forgive you."

"Thank you, Maddy. I love you, too."

She waved goodbye as her father drove out of the parking lot. Finally, after so many years of carrying the burden of her anger and heartbreak, God had lifted the weight from her shoulders.

* * *

Maddy had been begging her parents all summer to take her to the beach. Living in Arkansas, they were not close to the ocean by any stretch of the imagination, but somehow, Mom found a way.

One bright morning, they packed a small cooler with sandwiches, drinks, apples, and cookies. Mom threw a pile of towels in the trunk. They wore their swimsuits under their clothes and sandals on their feet. Then they drove an hour and a half to Beaver Lake.

Mom and Dad sang silly songs in the car and played the alphabet game and didn't complain when Maddy had to stop once to go to the bathroom, even though Mom had asked her to go three times before they left. When they got out of the car, Maddy was shocked to see a long stretch of sandy beach. "I thought you said Arkansas didn't have any beaches, Mom."

"I said Arkansas isn't on the ocean. This is just a lake, but it still has a pretty good beach."

Mom and Dad found a shaded picnic table to set their things down. They all peeled off their T-shirts. After they'd let Mom slather them with sunscreen, Maddy and Dad walked down to the water. Maddy kicked off her sandals. She didn't care if she had to walk on rocks.

The white, hot sun soaked through Maddy's clothes. The light turned her eyelids bright pink when she closed them. The heat bounced off the sand and pebbles, stinging her feet until they were red.

And then their feet met the water, green and dark and cool. Dad warned her again to watch out for sharp rocks, and she waded in slowly, letting her toes feel out the terrain below the lake.

Maddy had practiced treading water many times at her best friend's swimming pool. Now, she and Dad tried different strokes, swimming like frogs, swimming like mermaids, swimming like dogs. And then Mom joined in with her beautiful breaststroke, gliding through the water like a fish. They splashed and played until Maddy forgot to be careful and stubbed her toe.

Dad carried her to land, her toe cracked open and bleeding, and Mom bandaged it with supplies from the first-aid kit she always kept on hand. Then Maddy sat on the shore with her parents, and they built the biggest, most beautiful sandcastle

Maddy had ever seen, with turrets and battlements and a moat. And a mermaid Maddy built out of rocks and sticks and sand.

They were not the only family at the lake that day, but she felt as if they were in a bubble. Mom, Dad, and Maddy. They ate sandwiches and drank lemonade and read in the shade on their picnic bench. Dad kissed Mom on the lips when he thought Maddy wasn't looking. They listened to the music of the families around them. And, as always, Dad took pictures. Pictures of their sandcastle, pictures of the water, pictures of Maddy making silly faces, but mostly pictures of Mom.

When the sun hung low in the sky and Maddy's skin began to turn pink, Mom packed up the cooler and towels and dragged them to the car. Maddy fell asleep on the way home, but she dreamed of the lake. As she drifted off, she could hear her parents softly talking.

"Thanks for making this happen. I'm sorry things have been so tense lately."

"Me, too. Today was nice, though."

"I think we're going to make it, Cate. I still love you, no matter what."

"I love you, too, Henry. No matter what."

22

"*I* can't wait to see it!" Clara carried a salad bowl full of cucumbers and tomatoes fresh from her garden to the fellowship hall.

"Don't get your hopes too high." Madeleine held the door open for Clara and her mother, who carried a basket of wheat rolls.

"It'll be great, honey. I know it will." Catherine patted her on the shoulder with her free hand.

They dropped off their food at the tables set up in the fellowship hall and joined the small crowd gathered in front of Madeleine's mural. Madeleine watched as her aunt and mother admired the painting.

After finally finishing Matthew and making a couple adjustments, the rest of the painting had almost flowed out of her. The mural was divided into several scenes of Jesus interacting with people—the feeding of the 5,000; calming the storm; calling the disciples; and healing many people. In the middle of everything was a shadowed image of Jesus on the cross. Beams of light shone out from behind the cross, illuminating the vignettes surrounding it. And encircling the whole thing were the arms of God, as if He were drawing everyone closer to Himself. But the part Madeleine was most proud of …

"Hey! That's you!" Caitlin yelled, pointing to the mural and shoving Sophie with her other hand. "And that's me!"

She was right. Madeleine's style was certainly more impressionistic than realistic, but each of the faces on the mural belonged to someone from Shady Springs. Sophie's and Caitlin's likenesses were among the crowd Jesus fed, taking baskets of fish and bread. Clara, Julie, and Nancy could be seen receiving healing from Jesus. And A.J., Sam, and many of the other men from church were the disciples of Jesus.

"Wow, Maddy. This is really beautiful." Catherine pulled her close to her side as she admired the painting. "I'm so proud of you."

"Madeleine Mullins! You have outdone yourself." A.J. clapped her on the back as he walked up from behind. "I knew it was gonna be good, but you really did a great job."

"Thanks, A.J. I'm glad you like it." Madeleine smiled up at him.

"I don't just like it. I love it!" A.J. gave her shoulders a light squeeze. "A.J., good to see you!" Catherine patted A.J.'s arm. The two of them had grown pretty close in the weeks since Madeleine's baptism.

As A.J. chatted with Catherine, Madeleine caught Sam's eye across the crowd.

"I told you they would love it." Sam smiled broadly, opening his arms.

"I think you were right, as usual." Madeleine gave him a big hug. She was going to miss Sam when she headed home to Kansas City. He'd been a source of patient wisdom as Madeleine sorted through all of the many thoughts she had about God and the Bible. Thankfully, Sam had promised to answer any more questions that might pop up over phone or email.

After everyone had their fill of gazing at the mural, they moved into the fellowship hall. Almost the whole church had gathered for the dedication of the painting and a meal. Few could resist the draw of a potluck.

"I want to start by giving a big round of applause to Madeleine Mullins for the beautiful mural." Sam's voice boomed over the crowd.

Everyone clapped politely, except for the youth group who whooped and cheered as loud as possible. Madeleine ducked her head, embarrassed but flattered by the exuberant love the teens showed her.

"Please pray with me," Sam spoke over the din.

Madeleine couldn't help but keep her eyes open while Sam said a prayer of thanks for her, the mural, and the children of the congregation. She considered all the faces in the crowd. For the most part, she hadn't known any of them before she showed up in town in June. And now, they were some of the most important people in her life. People who forgave her and accepted her despite all her flaws.

She'd started out the summer lumping everyone from this church into the same category. Even when she began to learn the names of the people in the Shady Springs congregation, she still kept them all at a distance. But as the weeks went by and she spent more time with them, each face and each story stood out with clarity.

She was reminded of the mural on the wall. Her painting had started with unfocused splotches of color, meaningless to anyone except for her. But as the days passed and she put in more work, each portion of the mural grew in detail. Everything came into focus. She could no longer ignore the fact that the people here had their own unique stories and had changed her life in big and small ways. Madeleine's heart warmed at the love in the room.

After a satisfying meal and lots of conversation, the crowd began to thin. Families washed their dishes and loaded up their cars. Men and women wiped down the tables and chairs and stacked them along the walls. Finally, the only two people left were Madeleine and A.J. They turned off the lights and locked up the building before settling on the front steps.

Shady Springs was never very busy, and especially not at nine o'clock on a summer night. Madeleine and A.J. watched cars meander past the building to the town's only stoplight a few yards away. Fireflies flickered in the dim light, mimicking the blinking lights of headlights. The hot, sticky day had finally cooled, and Madeleine leaned back on her elbows. A soft breeze tickled her hair across her forehead.

"I've been thinking about what you suggested, about the Labor Day craft fair. I decided to reserve a booth to sell some of my paintings." Madeleine had called that morning and was told there were still a couple spots available. There was an upfront cost, but she hoped her sales would more than make up for it.

"Does that mean I'll get to see more of you this summer?" His voice sounded hopeful.

"Definitely. I will try to come every couple of weeks to visit Aunt Clara and ... everybody." Madeleine didn't know yet if she was allowed to say that A.J. was the person she really wanted to see this summer.

"You know how you asked if I've ever thought about being a preacher?"

"Yeah?" She picked a dandelion sprouting close to the steps and twirled it between her fingers.

"I've been giving it some more thought. And, well, I think that's what I want to do. Someday."

"Why not right now?"

A.J. chuckled. "Because I have to do some research and find a grad school and apply for scholarships. Slow down, Mullins." He elbowed her gently.

"Well, good." She inhaled the humid summer night air. "I'm glad you've finally found your calling."

"Madeleine, could I ask you something?" A.J. furrowed his brows. He was either angry or nervous about something.

Madeleine dropped the dandelion. Her stomach clenched. Something told her that whatever happened next would be very important. "Of course."

"I know we've been hanging out a lot this summer, but I was wondering ..." He fiddled with a blade of grass as he paused.

Madeleine's heart beat fast as she tried to be patient. Spit it out, already!

"Would you like to go on a date sometime?"

"Yes. I would like that." Madeleine turned to A.J. and practically laughed. "Of course, I would!" The thought that she might not was absolutely ridiculous.

"Oh, good." The poor guy looked so relieved, Madeleine wondered if he really had been nervous she would say no.

"A.J., you've got to know I like you very much." She met and held his gaze, willing him to believe her.

"I like you, too, Madeleine." And she knew it was true. In the way he went out of his way to spend time with her, the way he teased her, the way he looked at her. In fact, the way he looked at her right now was reason enough for her to believe him. Like he could kiss her that very minute.

And just as she had that thought, Madeleine realized she wanted to kiss A.J., too. She leaned closer, drawn in by the deep green of his eyes and the clean scent of his aftershave.

"May I kiss you?" he asked quietly.

Madeleine answered by pressing her lips to his. And it was absolutely perfect, colored with hues of warm goldenrod and bright rosy pink. She met his gaze.

"I'm glad I know you, Madeleine Mullins." He smiled down at her and planted another soft kiss on her forehead.

Her poor stomach couldn't take many more of his kisses tonight. She might never quiet the swarm of butterflies that had taken up residence there.

"You changed my life, A.J. Young. You and this church. I'm so thankful to you."

"I would do it all again."

And Madeleine would, too. She would do it all again to end up in the arms of her Heavenly Father and the arms of her earthly father, forgiven and forever changed.

DISCUSSION QUESTIONS

1. Did you grow up in a small town or a big city? What was your favorite part of your hometown?
2. Madeleine's experiences with the Church left her with a bad taste in her mouth and an aversion to Christianity. Have you ever tried to convince a friend or family member to come back to Christ? Have you ever heard Christians described as "hypocrites?"
3. Aunt Clara and Uncle George served as additional or even surrogate parents to Madeleine at times. Did you ever have friends or family members step into a special role in your life? Have you ever served as a mother or father figure to a child?
4. Do you think Madeleine forgave Nancy Jones too quickly? Or do you think she harbored resentment for too long? What would you have done in her situation?
5. At the end of the novel, Madeleine begins the path to reconciliation with her father. Do you think they will be able to patch their relationship?

6. Do you enjoy creating art like Madeleine? What is your creative outlet?

7. In chapter 18 Sam said, "Our very souls, our sense of justice, and our sense of beauty call out to Him (God)." Do you think that is true?

8. A.J. accuses Madeleine of being too sensitive when she can't let go of her anger with Mitchell and the youth group boys. Do you think she was? Have you ever been accused of being too emotional or too sensitive?

9. Did any characters from Shady Springs remind you of someone you know?

ACKNOWLEDGMENTS

It is a great privilege to be able to write acknowledgments two times for the same book! Thank you so much to those who read and loved Shady Springs the first time. And thanks to those who pestered me until I finally found a home for the whole series.

Linda, thank you so much for taking a risk on me. It's been a joy to work with you.

I'm eternally grateful to Amy Anguish and Rachel Herod, my critique partners and dear friends. You brought me from aspiring writer to published author. I love you ladies!

Thank you to all of my early readers, especially Rebecca Vinzant, Tina Robison, Maydell Yeakley, and Rose Landon. And thank you to Carol Vinzant for inspiring me with your novel.

Michael, I'm delighted you finally read my book and actually liked it! You encouraged me to write from the beginning and watched our crazy kids so I could do it. You're the best.

To you, the reader, a very big thanks to you for choosing Shady Springs. I hope this book has been a blessing to you.

To the Creator God from whom all creativity flows, I pray that my work always and only glorifies You.

ABOUT THE AUTHOR

Sarah Anne Crouch aims to bless readers with inspirational fiction brimming with heart. The author of A Summer in Shady Springs, "A Sweet Dream Come True" from the Love in Any Season collection, and "Where Love is Planted" from the Love Delivered collection, Sarah writes stories featuring characters growing in love and their relationships with God.

Although Sarah always wanted to be an author, she spent time as a fifth-grade English teacher, earned a degree in library science, and currently makes feeble attempts to corral her children as a stay-at-home mom.

Sarah has lived in many places but calls Arkansas home and draws inspiration from the beautiful surroundings of the Natural State. A graduate of Harding University, she remains actively involved with her alma mater.

Outside of writing, Sarah enjoys reading books, exploring recipes, playing piano music, and cherishing emails from her readers.

A Match Made at Christmas

A novella collection—includes "A Match of Her Own"

by Sarah Anne Crouch

A-parent-ly Christmas (by **Amy R Anguish**)—Noel and Joy Davidson didn't mean to separate, but a job promotion and educational opportunities were too much for their marriage to withstand. Now, it's Christmas and their son Andy wants them together. Between his mischief, an unexpected snowstorm, and the holiday spirit, they're remembering why they first wanted to be together. But which one will give up their dream for the other?

A Match of her Own (by **Sarah Anne Crouch**)—Victoria Wood is torn between elation and devastation now that her sister is married and gone. When she realizes her sister's best friend is alone and best-friend-less on Christmas, she knows just what to do. Set her up with a boyfriend! But pesky Jared Knight keeps getting in the way. Jared can't date Victoria—she's too immature—but he can't convince his heart to move on. How will he keep Victoria from ruining everyone's love lives? When will she realize her perfect match is closer than she thinks?

Jingle Bell Matchmakers (by **Lori DeJong**)—When country music star Aubrey Mayfield is lured home after years away, she's bewildered when she and ex-fiance-now-widowed-dad Cody Lansdale keep finding themselves in the same place at the same time. As they become reacquainted, however, old feelings stir. Aubrey's at a crossroads in her career and is contemplating a change. But when a chance at headlining her own tour takes her back to Nashville, Cody realizes her dreams may once again come between them. Unless God, with a little help from the Jingle Bell Committee, has a better plan.

The Santa Setup (by **Heather Greer**)—Turning friendship into love takes magic. Good thing Nicholas Eckert and Julie Clarke work at Christmas Wonderland. The attraction brims with holiday magic, not to mention four teenage elves determined that Mr. and Mrs. Claus stop playing a couple and become one. The teens will need more than mistletoe to pair up these two. Julie is seeing someone, and Nick won't risk their friendship for possible love. Only the elven employees' outrageous antics stand a chance of setting up Santa in time for Christmas.

Get your copy here:

https://scrivenings.link/amatchmadeatchristmas

* * *

Love Delivered

A novella collection—includes "Where Love Is Planted"

by Sarah Anne Crouch

Romance at Register Five (by Amy R Anguish)—Mack McDonald isn't happy about the Grocerease app coming to his grocery store. But he's committed to the sixty-day trial period, and braces himself to lose money. Kaitlyn Daniels loves how the Grocerease app helps her make ends meet so she can assist her mom, the reason she moved to small Sassafras, AR. Mack and Kaitlyn struggle to overcome differing opinions on the perks of the app. But if they don't, it could keep them from something even better.

Where Love is Planted (by Sarah Anne Crouch)—Ivy Aaronson is surrounded by family at their flower shop in West Texas—just the way she likes it. But she's given up hope on ever finding a man who understands her choices. When attorney Grant Keller orders flowers for his mother, Ivy wonders if maybe there are indeed some considerate men left in the world…until she finds out Grant's relationship with his parents is less than ideal. How can Ivy ever find love when every man she meets puts career over family?

Sweet Delivery (by Heather Greer)—After winning Cake That, Will Forrester thinks his Pastry Perfect Baking Dreams have come true. The sweetness fades when a chain bakery moves to town, and Will must adjust his plans to keep his customers. Hiring Erica Gerard is one of those changes. As they work together, Erica challenges Will and offers new ideas to improve the bakery. Soon, Erica and Will start bringing out the best in each other. But Erica harbors a secret, and if it's discovered, Will might never be the same.

***The Mermaids, the Ex, and USSS* (by Rachel Herod)**—Braig Sanborn is the most loyal employee the United States Shipping Service has ever seen, which is why he agreed to transfer across the country with only a few weeks' notice. Bailey Bivens is so busy planning a friend's wedding, she didn't expect to fall for the carrier who delivers packages to her house. When they both find themselves in too deep, will they agree the relationship was doomed from the start?

Get your copy here:

https://scrivenings.link/lovedelivered

* * *

Love in Any Season

A novella collection—includes "A Sweet Dream Come True"

by Sarah Anne Crouch

Spring Has Sprung(by **Regina Rudd Merrick**)—Laurel Pascal, Assistant City Manager of Spring, Kentucky, is tasked with organizing the town's beloved Daffodil Festival, and she's not happy. An allergy sufferer all her life, she dreads the season from the first Daffodil bloom in the yard to the last coat of pollen on her car. Newcomer Dr. Owen Roswell volunteers to help, and soon finds that not only does Laurel need his expertise as an allergist, but help in appreciating the season she's obligated to celebrate.

What does he want more—for Laurel to fall in love with his favorite season? Or him?

The Missing Piece (by **Amy R. Anguish**)—Beth Norton and Tommy England grew up together with best-friend moms who had a love of quilting and a business celebrating the craft. When high school ended, though, so did Beth and Tommy's friendship.

When Tommy moves back after seven years and his mother's death, he can't understand why Beth is so angry with him. Helping Beth and her mother stabilize the finances of the business, they're forced to work together. As Tommy sorts through his mother's things, he finds an unfinished quilt, and it turns into a joint project.

With each stitch taken, they work toward more than just a completed blanket.

A Sweet Dream Come True (by **Sarah Anne Crouch**)—Isaac Campbell is living his dream of running an ice cream shop but fears he won't last past the first difficult year. Mel Wilson is a busy single mother who longs to be a chocolatier but is too afraid to turn her dreams into reality.

When Mel and Isaac meet at Bestwood, Tennessee's fall festival, it seems like divine providence. But once Mel agrees to help Isaac bring in customers by selling her chocolates at his shop, she realizes how challenging running a business can be.

Can Mel and Isaac trust in God's provision and make a leap of faith?

Will their partnership end in disaster, or will it be a sweet dream come true?

Sugar and Spice (by **Heather Greer**)—Emeline Becker, owner of Sugar and Spice Bakery, loves New Kuchenbrünn, except for the gingerbread. As the only bakery, she supplies the annual Gingerbread Festival with the one treat she can't stand. It's gingerbread everywhere.

Things get worse when Ryker Lehmann is hired as the festival photographer. He was her secret teen crush, her sister's boyfriend, and witness to her worst humiliation. Plus, he broke her sister's heart and bruised hers when he left town after graduation. Now, he's back in town, determined to fix their friendship before the festival ends.

With gingerbread and Ryker together, can Emmie make it through the festival with her mind and heart intact?

Get your copy here:

https://scrivenings.link/loveinanyseason

* * *

Scrivenings
PRESS
Quench your thirst for story.
www.ScriveningsPress.com

Stay up-to-date on your favorite books and authors with our free e-newsletters.

ScriveningsPress.com